that's so raven

SERIES CREATED BY
MICHAEL PORYES AND SUSAN SHERMAN

THE TROUBLE WITH BOYS

TOKYOPOP®

HAMBURG · LONDON · LOS ANGELES · TOKYO

Contributing Editors - Robert Buscemi & Ivy Garcia
Graphic Design & Lettering - Monalisa J. de Asis, Tomás Montalvo-Lagos
Cover Layout - Ray Makowski

Editor - Erin Stein
Managing Editor - Jill Freshney
Production Coordinator - Antonio DePietro
Production Manager - Jennifer Miller
Art Director - Matt Alford
Editorial Director - Jeremy Ross
VP of Production - Ron Klamert
President & C.O.O. - John Parker
Publisher & C.E.O. - Stuart Levy

Come visit us online at www.TOKYOPOP.com

A TOKYOPOP® Cine-Manga® Book
TOKYOPOP Inc.
5900 Wilshire Blvd., Suite 2000, Los Angeles, CA 90036

That's So Raven Volume 2: The Trouble with Boys
© 2004 Disney Enterprises, Inc.

ISBN: 1-59182-807-4
First TOKYOPOP printing: October 2004

10 9 8 7 6 5 4 3 2

Printed in the USA

THE TROUBLE WITH BOYS

CONTENTS

WHO'S WHO

RAVEN

A typical teenage girl who's also a psychic, although the future never seems to turn out like she thinks it will.

EDDIE

Raven's best friend.

CHELSEA

One of Raven's closest friends.

CORY

Raven's little brother.

VICTOR

Raven's dad.

TANYA

Raven's mom.

A DOG BY ANY OTHER NAME

WRITTEN BY
MICHAEL PORYES AND SUSAN SHERMAN

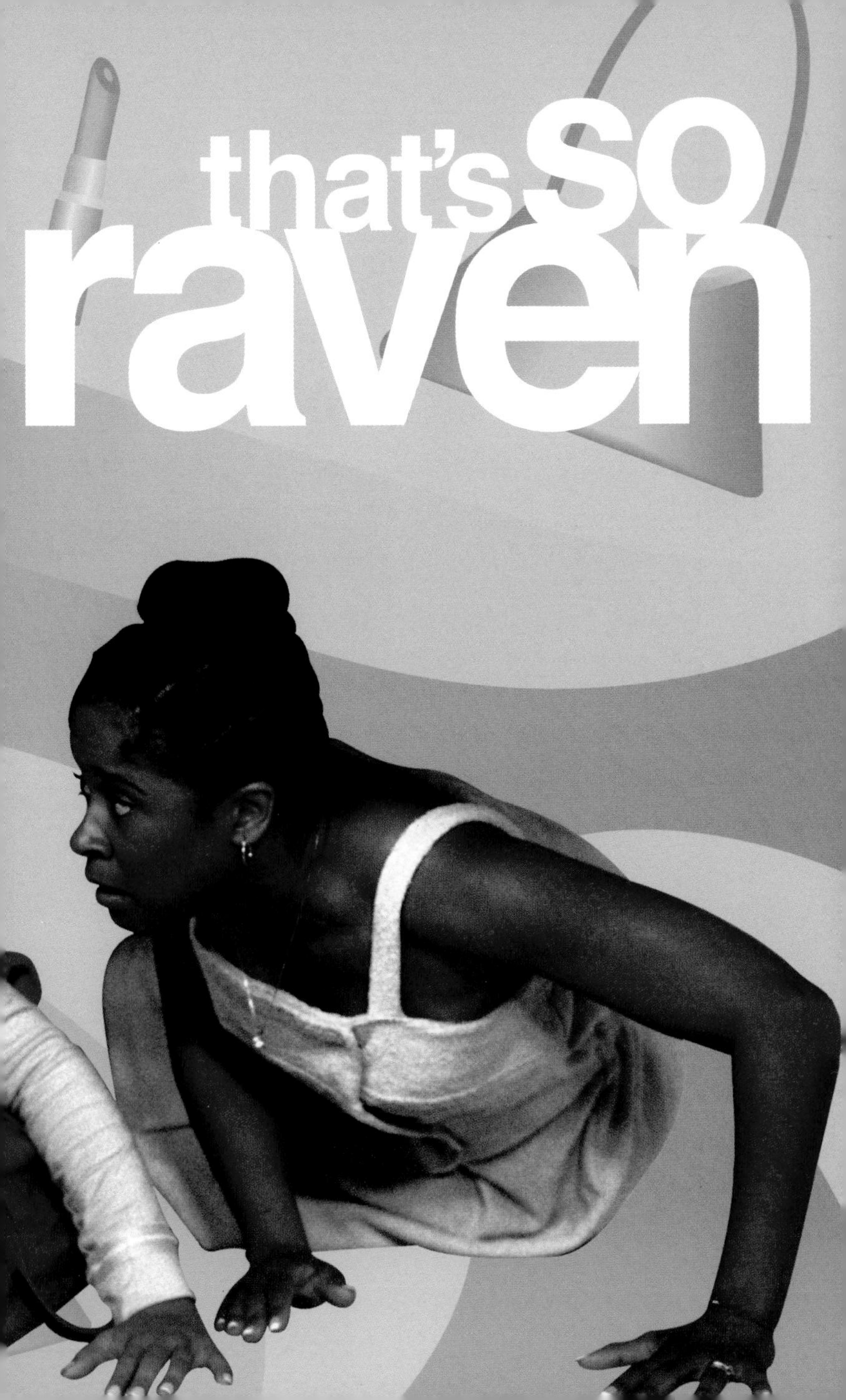
that's so
raven

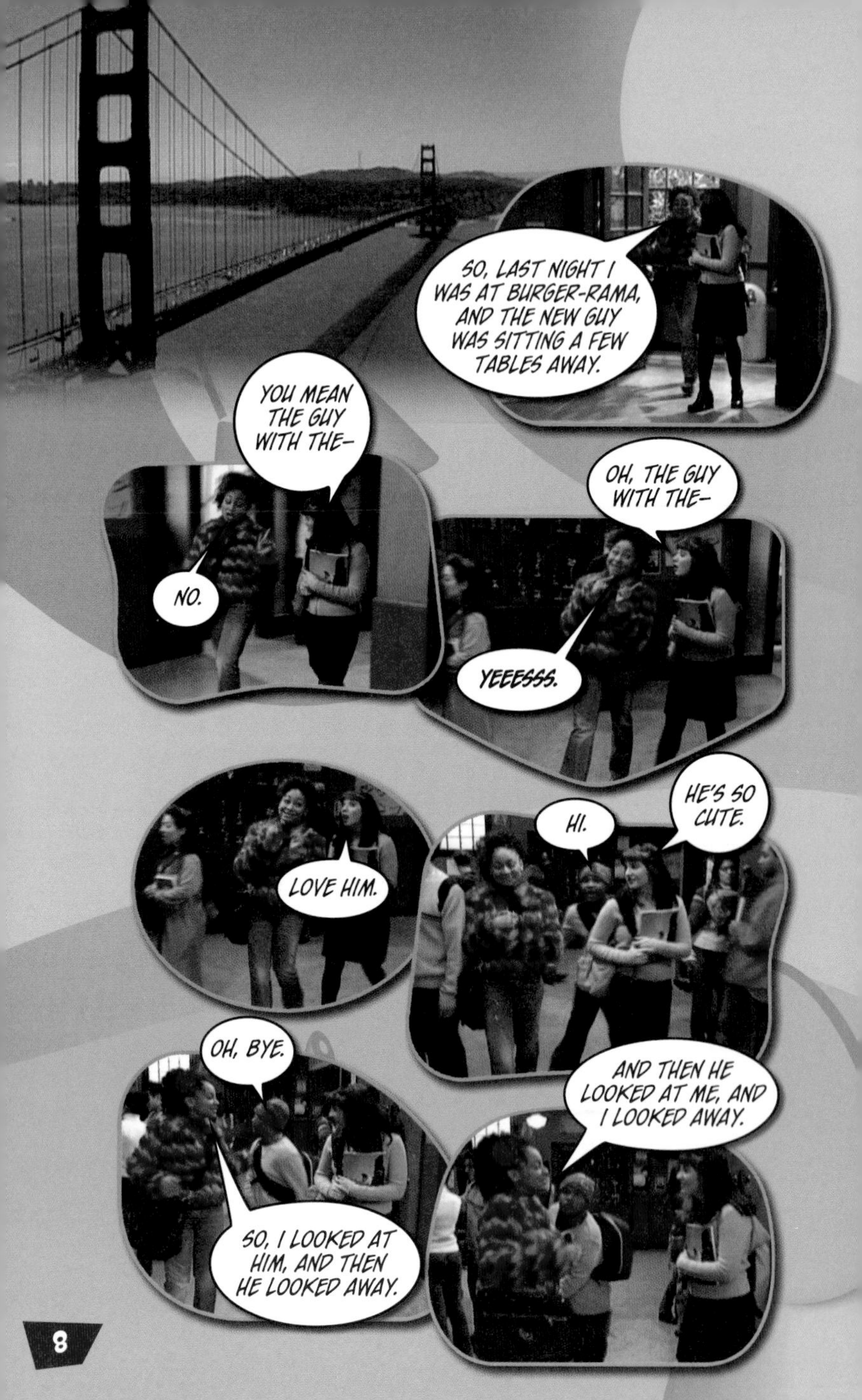

SO, LAST NIGHT I WAS AT BURGER-RAMA, AND THE NEW GUY WAS SITTING A FEW TABLES AWAY.
YOU MEAN THE GUY WITH THE-
NO.
OH, THE GUY WITH THE-
YEEESSS.
LOVE HIM.
HI.
HE'S SO CUTE.
OH, BYE.
SO, I LOOKED AT HIM, AND THEN HE LOOKED AWAY.
AND THEN HE LOOKED AT ME, AND I LOOKED AWAY.

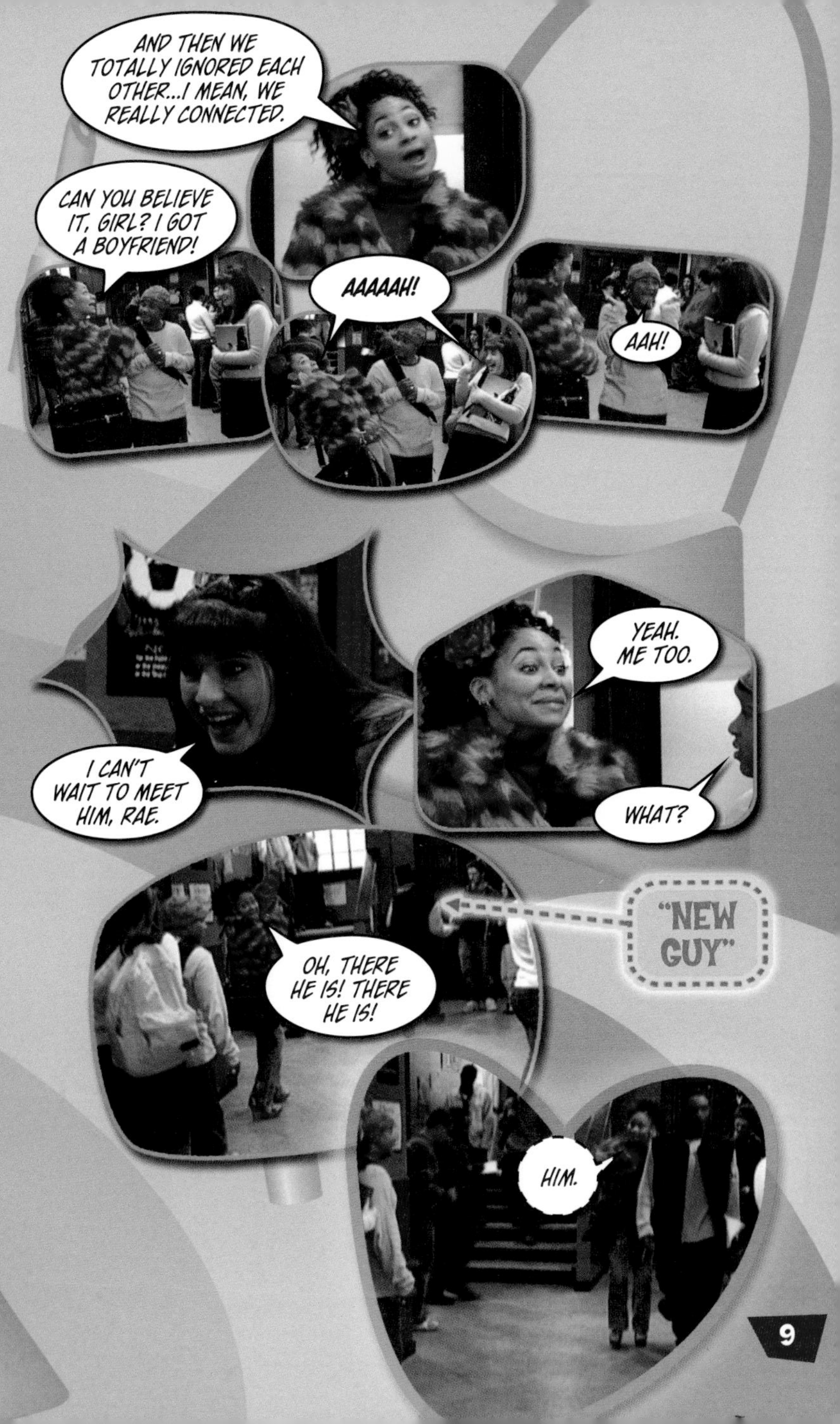
AND THEN WE TOTALLY IGNORED EACH OTHER...I MEAN, WE REALLY CONNECTED.
CAN YOU BELIEVE IT, GIRL? I GOT A BOYFRIEND!
AAAAAH!
AAH!
I CAN'T WAIT TO MEET HIM, RAE.
YEAH. ME TOO.
WHAT?
OH, THERE HE IS! THERE HE IS!
"NEW GUY"
HIM.

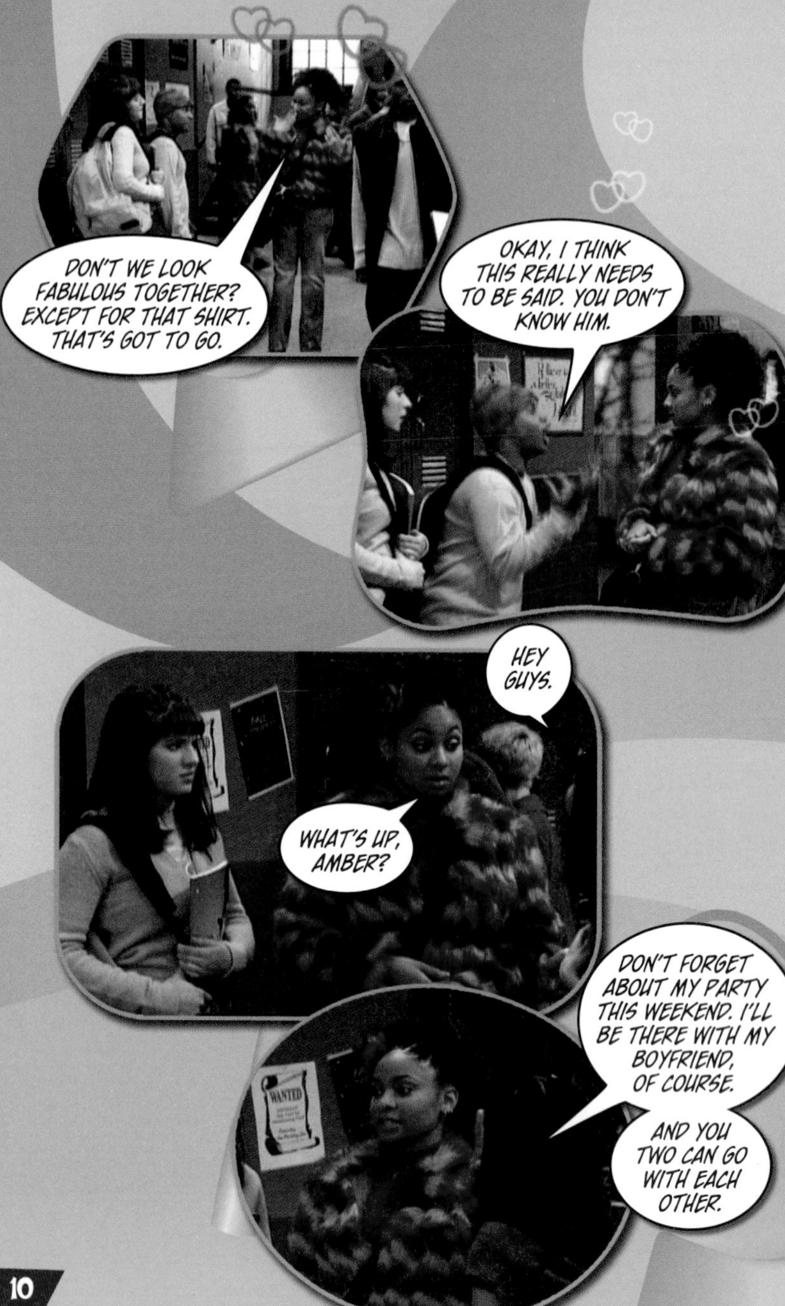
DON'T WE LOOK FABULOUS TOGETHER? EXCEPT FOR THAT SHIRT. THAT'S GOT TO GO.
OKAY, I THINK THIS REALLY NEEDS TO BE SAID. YOU DON'T KNOW HIM.
HEY GUYS.
WHAT'S UP, AMBER?
DON'T FORGET ABOUT MY PARTY THIS WEEKEND. I'LL BE THERE WITH MY BOYFRIEND, OF COURSE.
AND YOU TWO CAN GO WITH EACH OTHER.

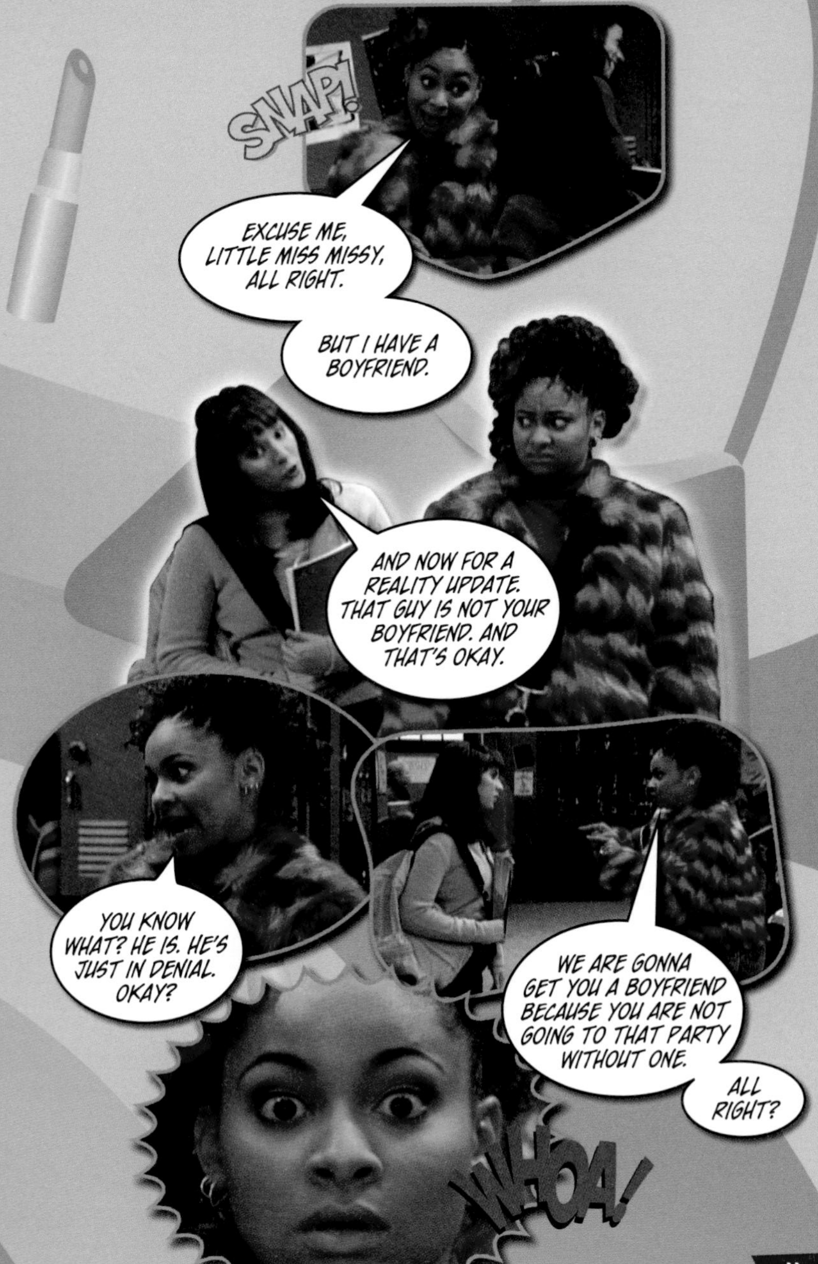
SNAP!
EXCUSE ME, LITTLE MISS MISSY, ALL RIGHT.
BUT I HAVE A BOYFRIEND.
AND NOW FOR A REALITY UPDATE. THAT GUY IS NOT YOUR BOYFRIEND. AND THAT'S OKAY.
YOU KNOW WHAT? HE IS. HE'S JUST IN DENIAL. OKAY?
WE ARE GONNA GET YOU A BOYFRIEND BECAUSE YOU ARE NOT GOING TO THAT PARTY WITHOUT ONE.
ALL RIGHT?
WHOA!

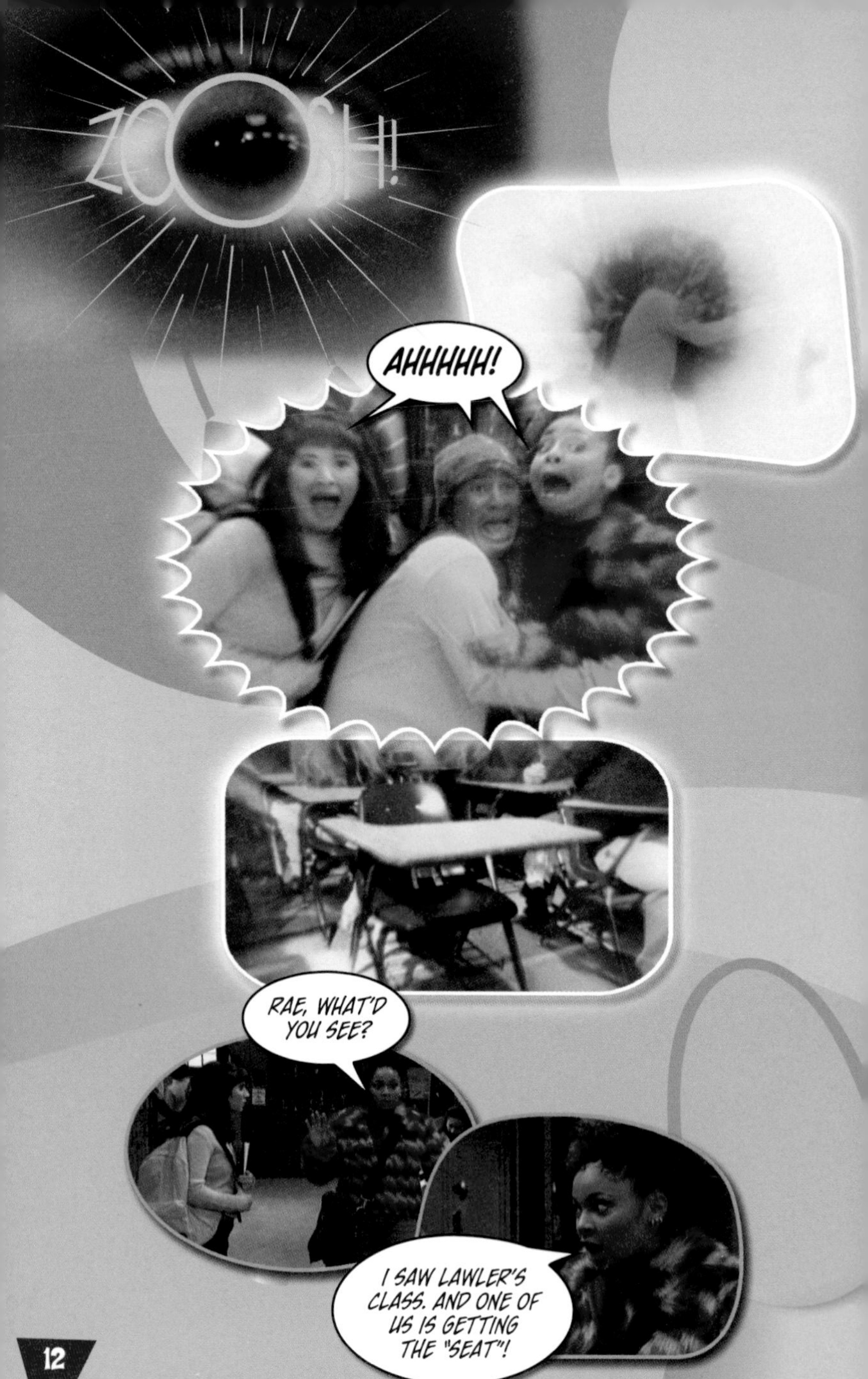
ZOOOSH!
AHHHHH!
RAE, WHAT'D YOU SEE?
I SAW LAWLER'S CLASS. AND ONE OF US IS GETTING THE "SEAT"!

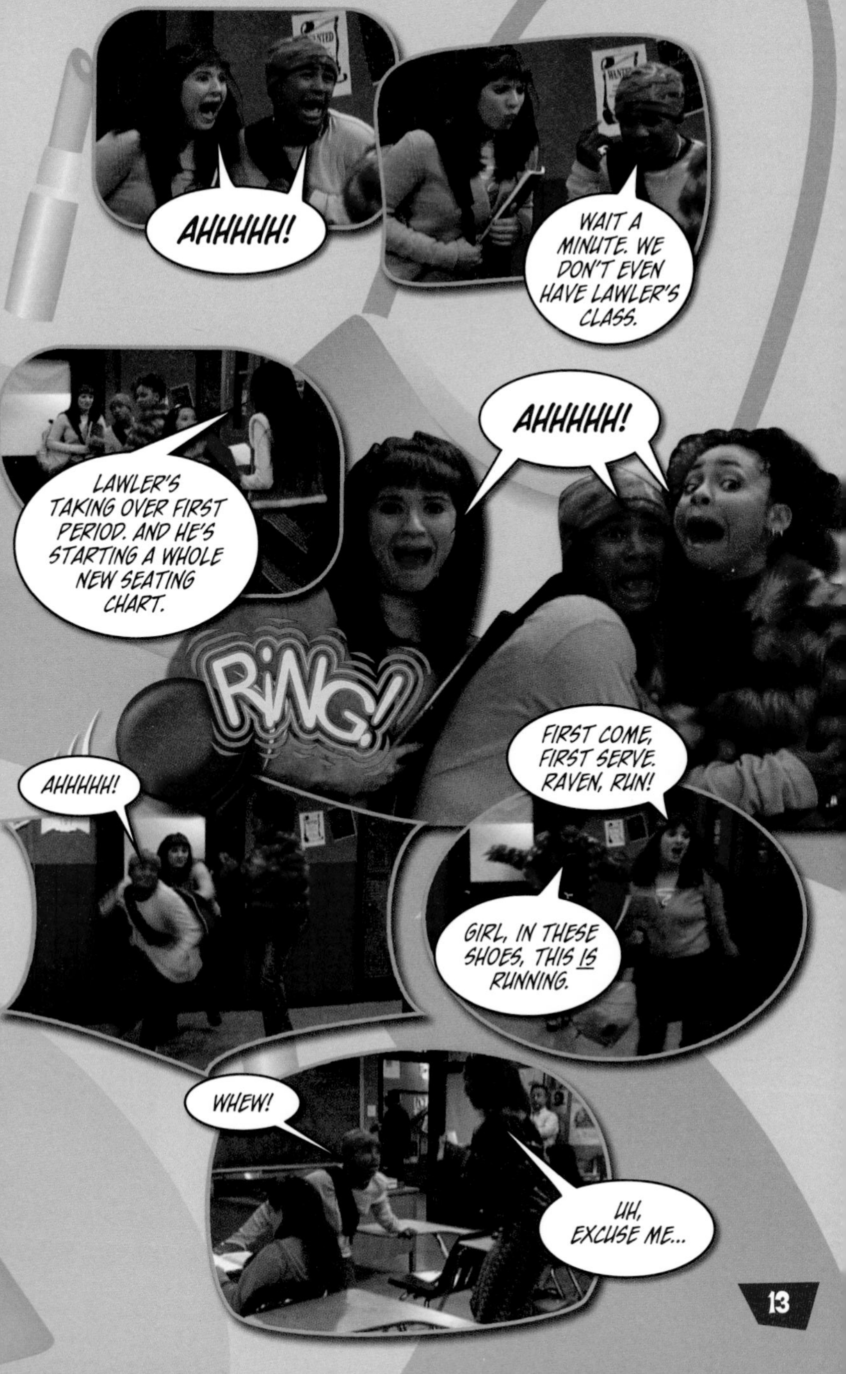
AHHHHH!
WAIT A MINUTE. WE DON'T EVEN HAVE LAWLER'S CLASS.
LAWLER'S TAKING OVER FIRST PERIOD. AND HE'S STARTING A WHOLE NEW SEATING CHART.
AHHHHH!
RING!
AHHHHH!
FIRST COME, FIRST SERVE. RAVEN, RUN!
GIRL, IN THESE SHOES, THIS IS RUNNING.
WHEW!
UH, EXCUSE ME...

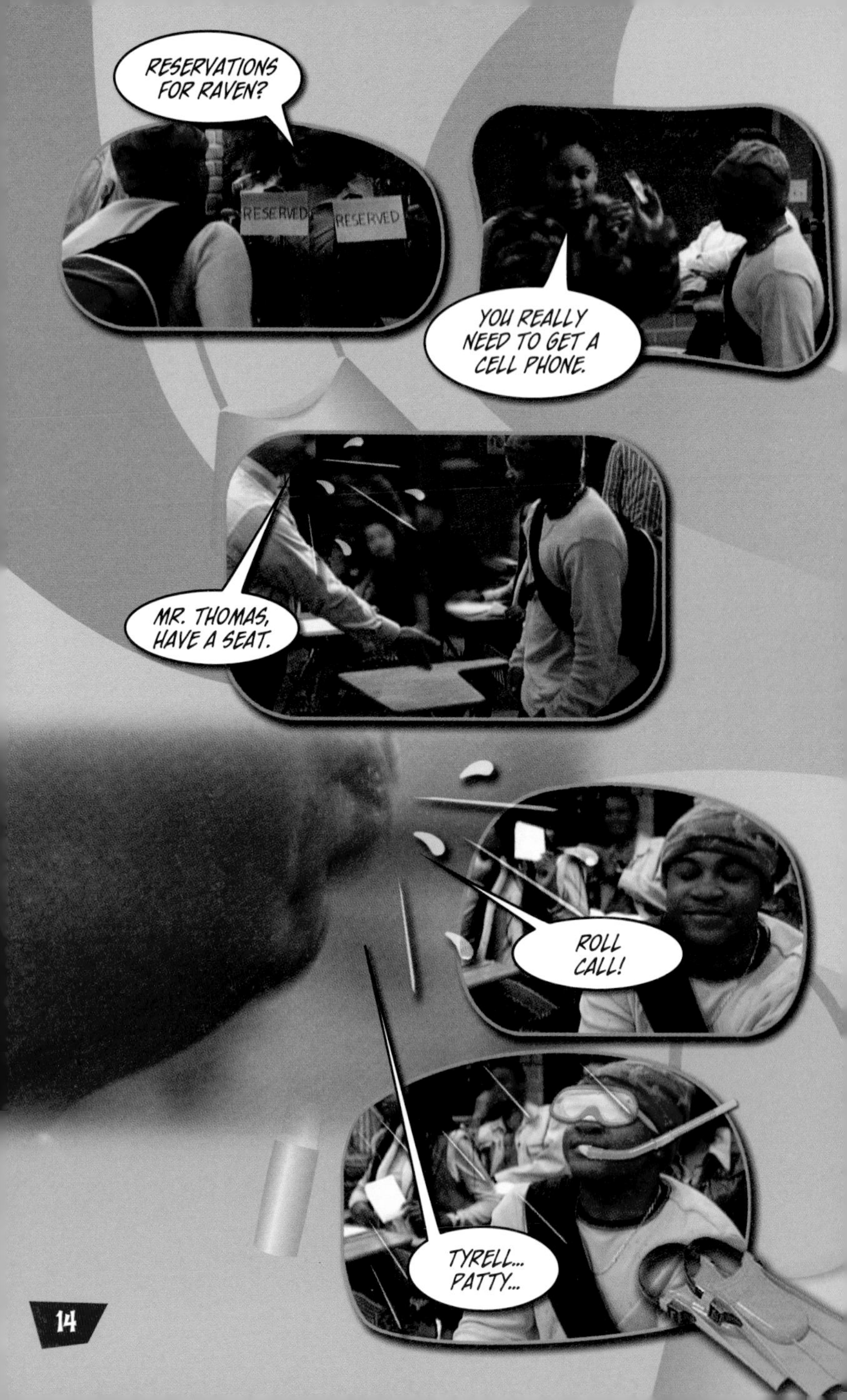
RESERVATIONS FOR RAVEN?
RESERVED
RESERVED
YOU REALLY NEED TO GET A CELL PHONE.
MR. THOMAS, HAVE A SEAT.
ROLL CALL!
TYRELL... PATTY...

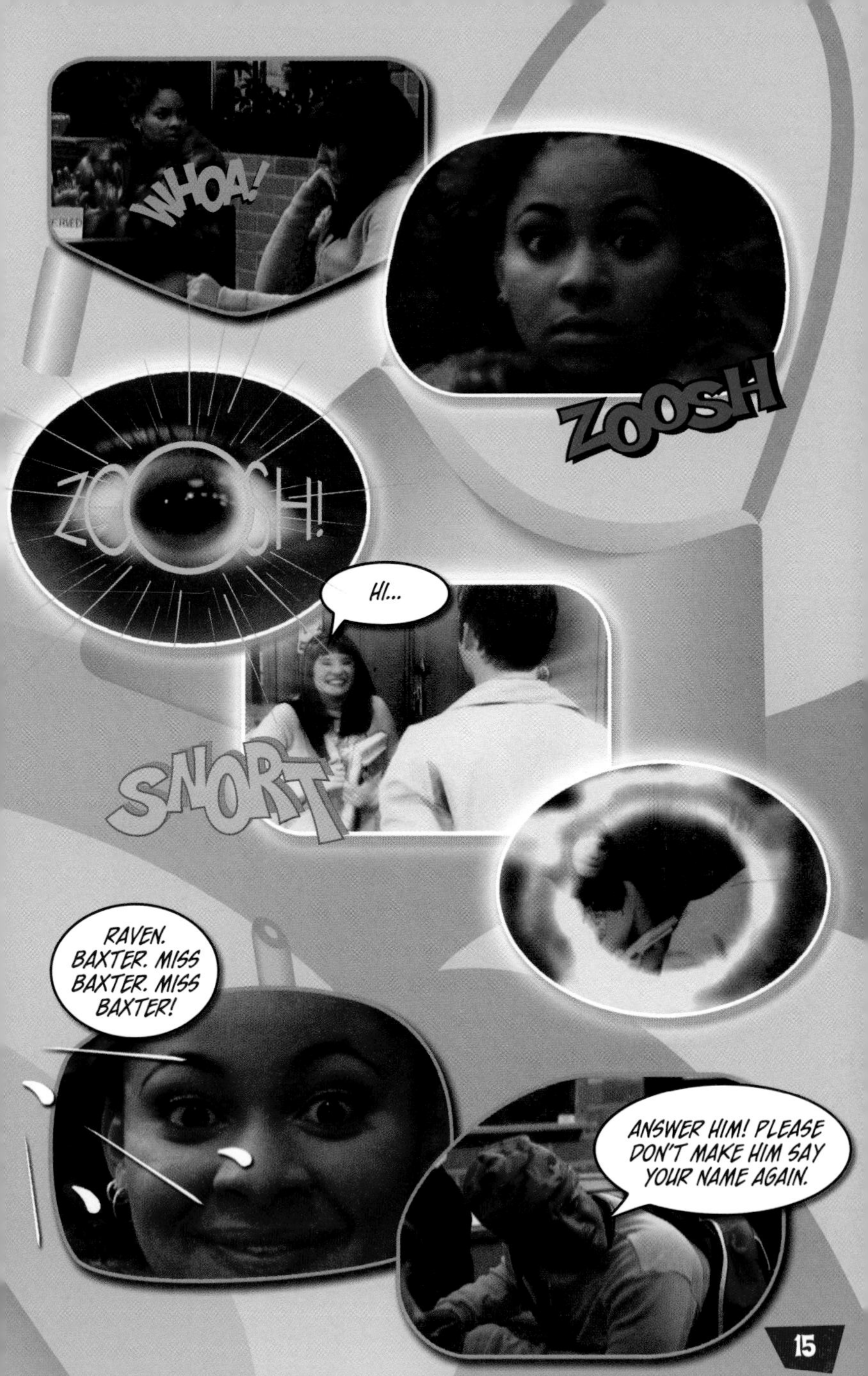
WHOA!
ZOOSH
ZOOSH!
HI...
SNORT
RAVEN. BAXTER. MISS BAXTER. MISS BAXTER!
ANSWER HIM! PLEASE DON'T MAKE HIM SAY YOUR NAME AGAIN.

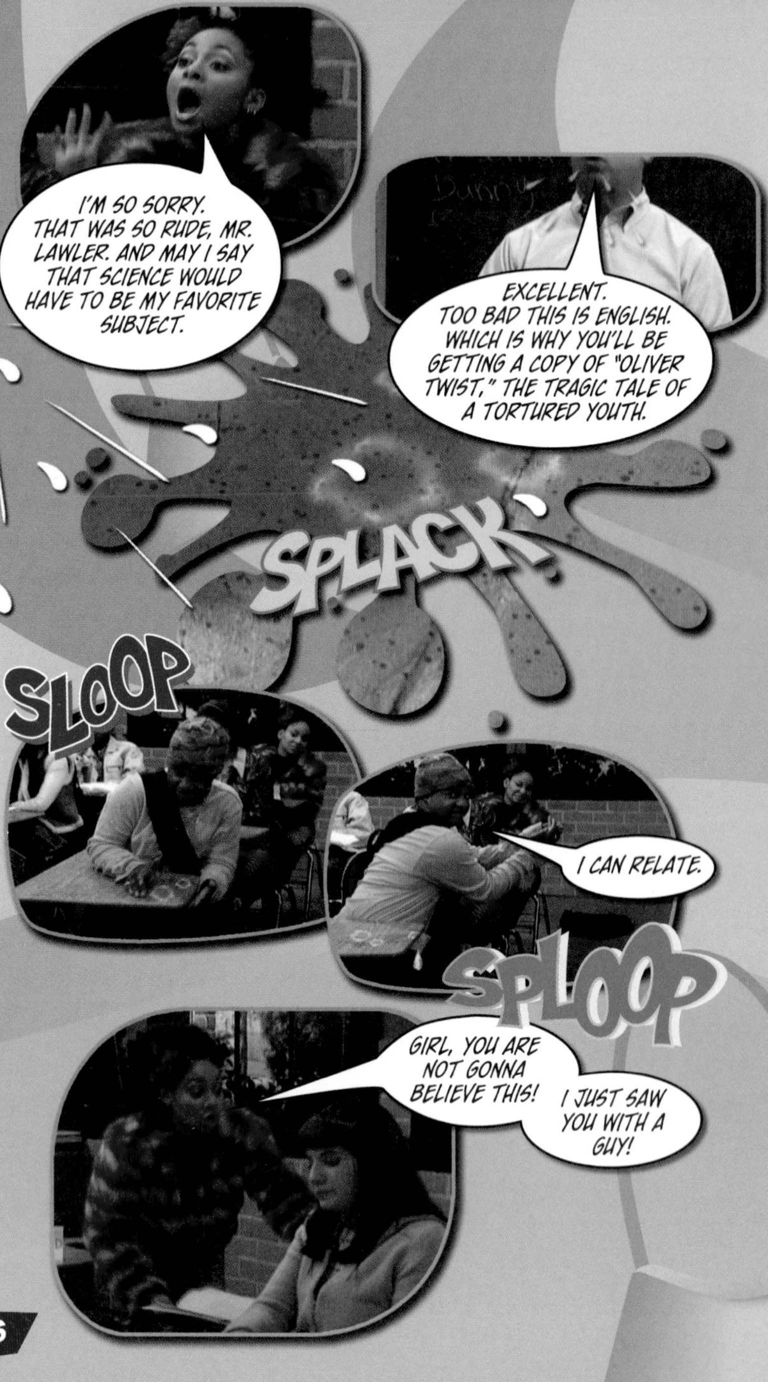
I'M SO SORRY. THAT WAS SO RUDE, MR. LAWLER. AND MAY I SAY THAT SCIENCE WOULD HAVE TO BE MY FAVORITE SUBJECT.
EXCELLENT. TOO BAD THIS IS ENGLISH. WHICH IS WHY YOU'LL BE GETTING A COPY OF "OLIVER TWIST," THE TRAGIC TALE OF A TORTURED YOUTH.
SPLACK
SLOOP
I CAN RELATE.
SPLOOP
GIRL, YOU ARE NOT GONNA BELIEVE THIS!
I JUST SAW YOU WITH A GUY!

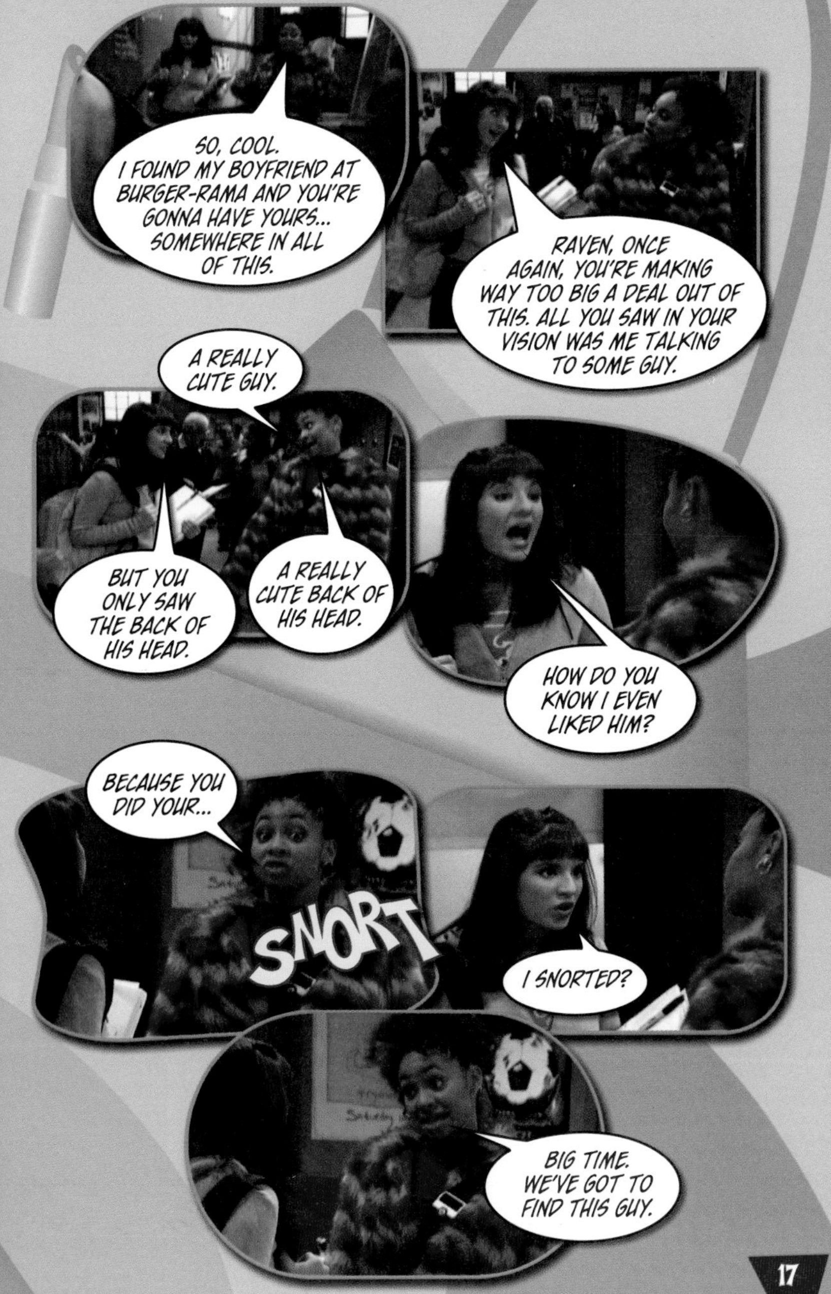
SO, COOL. I FOUND MY BOYFRIEND AT BURGER-RAMA AND YOU'RE GONNA HAVE YOURS... SOMEWHERE IN ALL OF THIS.
RAVEN, ONCE AGAIN, YOU'RE MAKING WAY TOO BIG A DEAL OUT OF THIS. ALL YOU SAW IN YOUR VISION WAS ME TALKING TO SOME GUY.
A REALLY CUTE GUY.
BUT YOU ONLY SAW THE BACK OF HIS HEAD.
A REALLY CUTE BACK OF HIS HEAD.
HOW DO YOU KNOW I EVEN LIKED HIM?
BECAUSE YOU DID YOUR...
SNORT
I SNORTED?
BIG TIME. WE'VE GOT TO FIND THIS GUY.

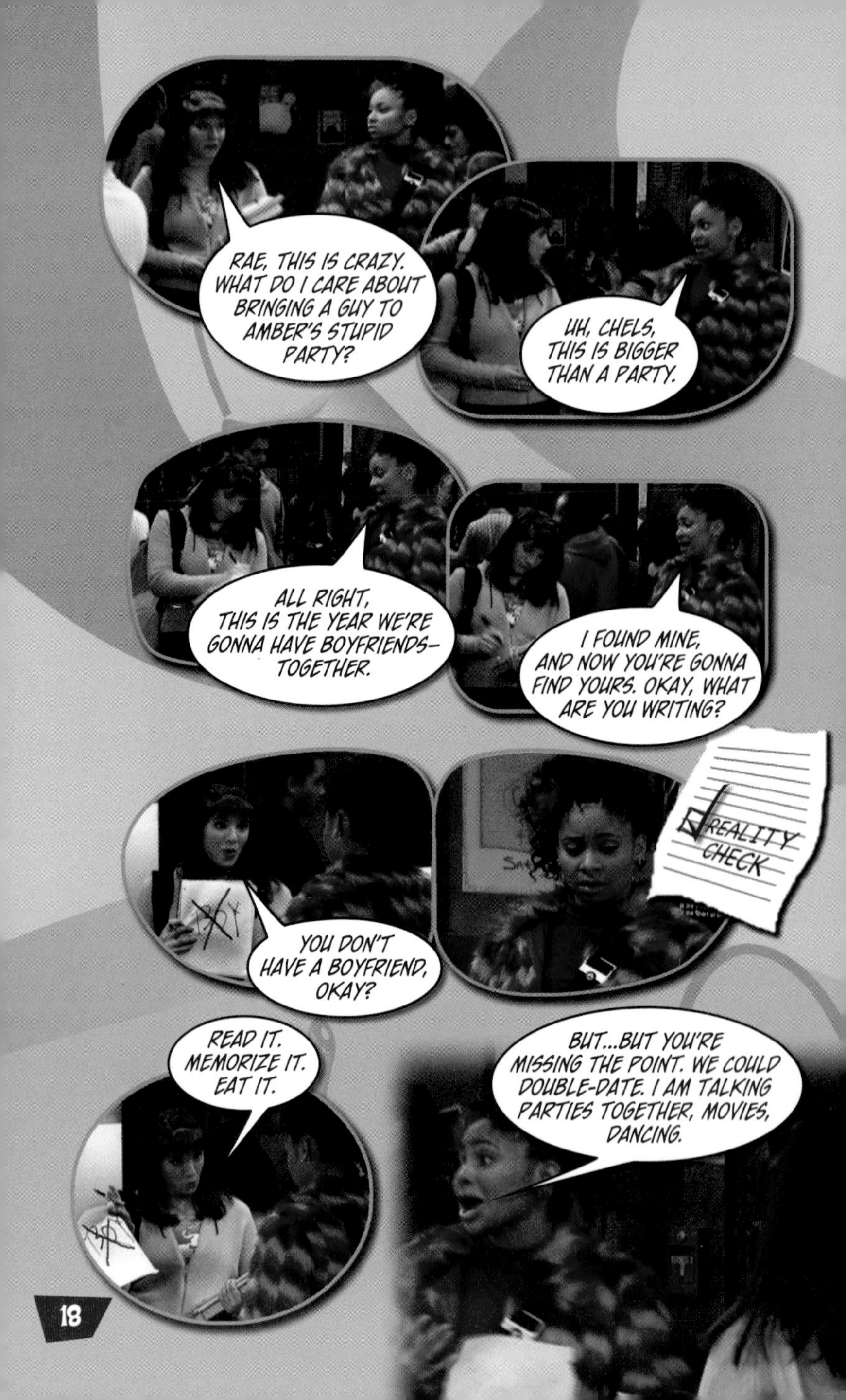
RAE, THIS IS CRAZY. WHAT DO I CARE ABOUT BRINGING A GUY TO AMBER'S STUPID PARTY?
UH, CHELS, THIS IS BIGGER THAN A PARTY.
ALL RIGHT, THIS IS THE YEAR WE'RE GONNA HAVE BOYFRIENDS— TOGETHER.
I FOUND MINE, AND NOW YOU'RE GONNA FIND YOURS. OKAY, WHAT ARE YOU WRITING?
YOU DON'T HAVE A BOYFRIEND, OKAY?
REALITY CHECK
READ IT. MEMORIZE IT. EAT IT.
BUT...BUT YOU'RE MISSING THE POINT. WE COULD DOUBLE-DATE. I AM TALKING PARTIES TOGETHER, MOVIES, DANCING.

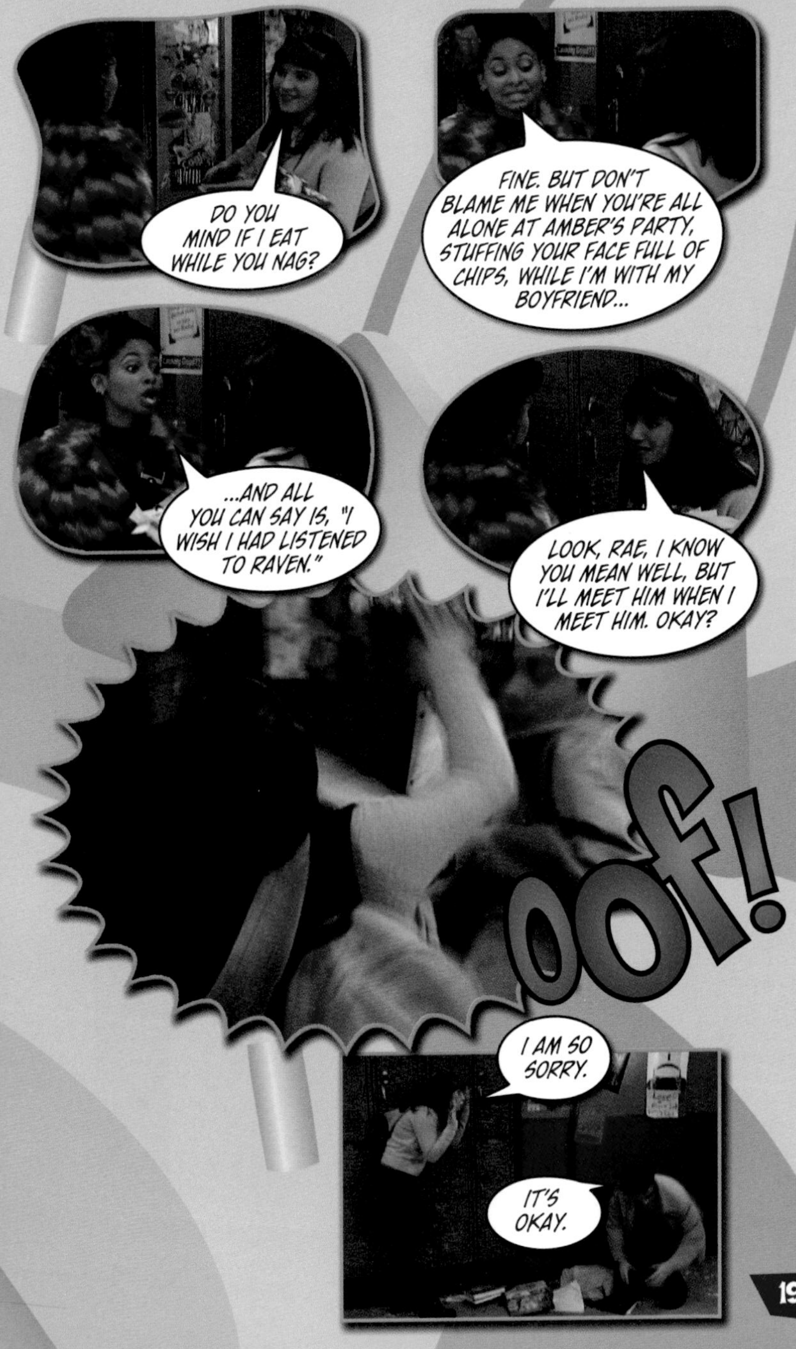
DO YOU MIND IF I EAT WHILE YOU NAG?
FINE. BUT DON'T BLAME ME WHEN YOU'RE ALL ALONE AT AMBER'S PARTY, STUFFING YOUR FACE FULL OF CHIPS, WHILE I'M WITH MY BOYFRIEND...
...AND ALL YOU CAN SAY IS, "I WISH I HAD LISTENED TO RAVEN."
LOOK, RAE, I KNOW YOU MEAN WELL, BUT I'LL MEET HIM WHEN I MEET HIM. OKAY?
OOF!
I AM SO SORRY.
IT'S OKAY.

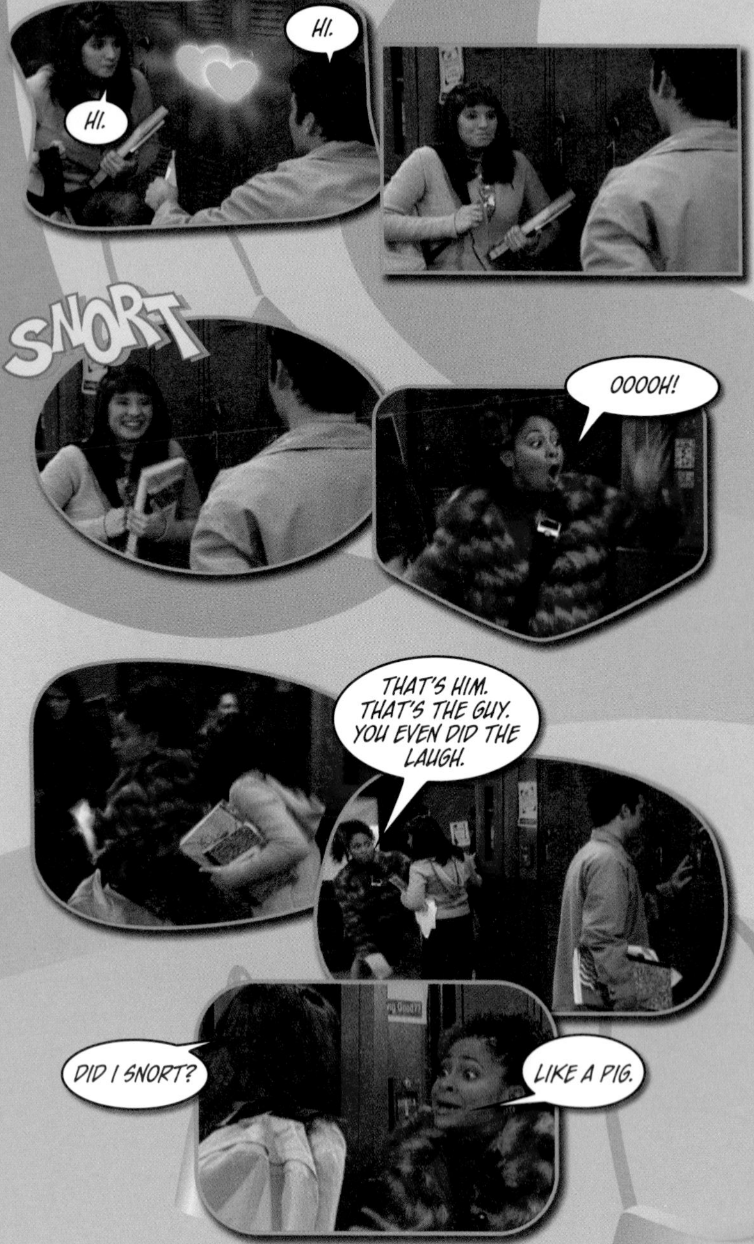
HI.
HI.
SNORT
OOOOH!
THAT'S HIM. THAT'S THE GUY. YOU EVEN DID THE LAUGH.
DID I SNORT?
LIKE A PIG.

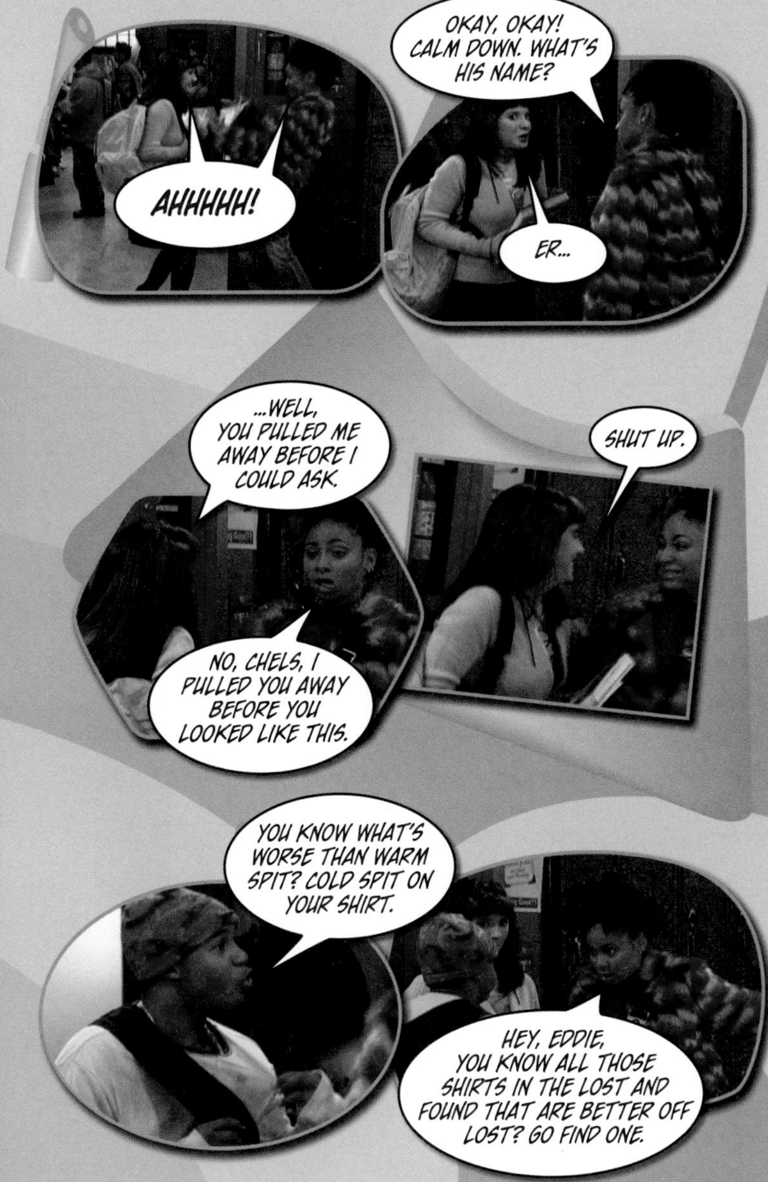
AHHHHH!
OKAY, OKAY! CALM DOWN. WHAT'S HIS NAME?
ER...
...WELL, YOU PULLED ME AWAY BEFORE I COULD ASK.
NO, CHELS, I PULLED YOU AWAY BEFORE YOU LOOKED LIKE THIS.
SHUT UP.
YOU KNOW WHAT'S WORSE THAN WARM SPIT? COLD SPIT ON YOUR SHIRT.
HEY, EDDIE, YOU KNOW ALL THOSE SHIRTS IN THE LOST AND FOUND THAT ARE BETTER OFF LOST? GO FIND ONE.

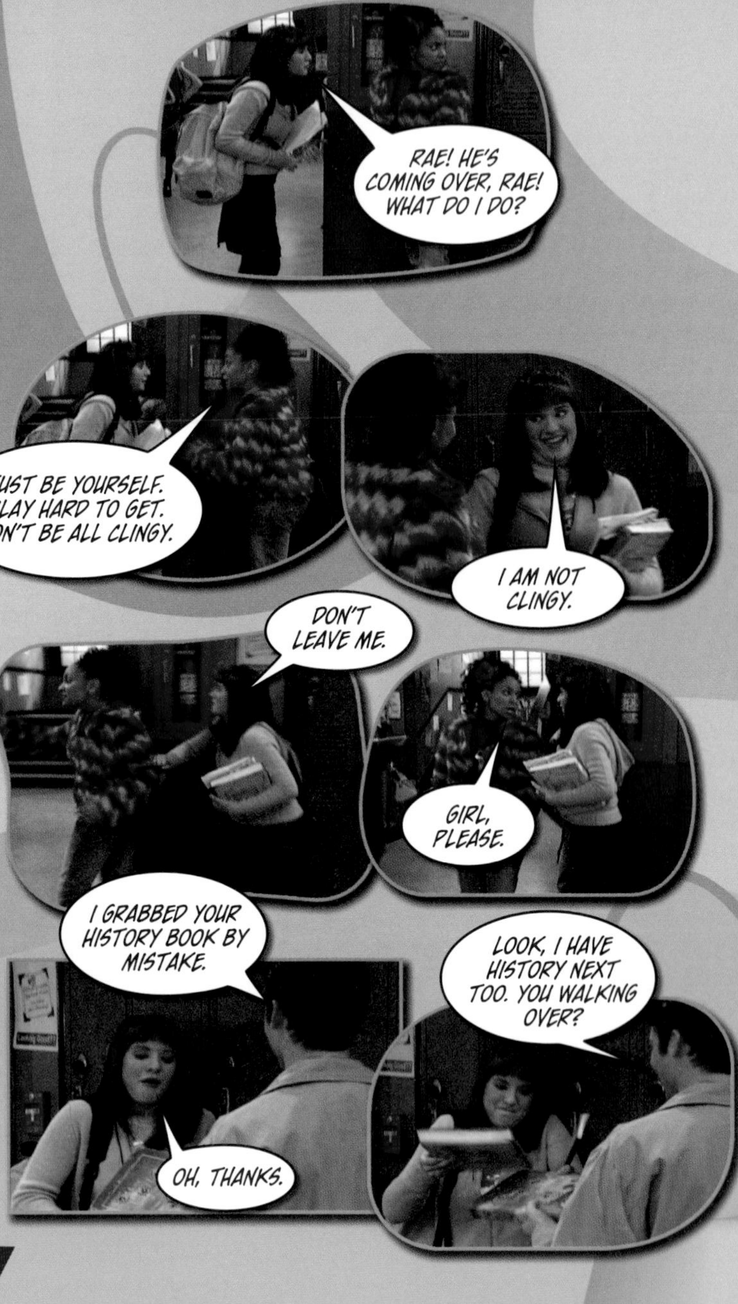
RAE! HE'S COMING OVER, RAE! WHAT DO I DO?
JUST BE YOURSELF. PLAY HARD TO GET. DON'T BE ALL CLINGY.
I AM NOT CLINGY.
DON'T LEAVE ME.
GIRL, PLEASE.
I GRABBED YOUR HISTORY BOOK BY MISTAKE.
OH, THANKS.
LOOK, I HAVE HISTORY NEXT TOO. YOU WALKING OVER?

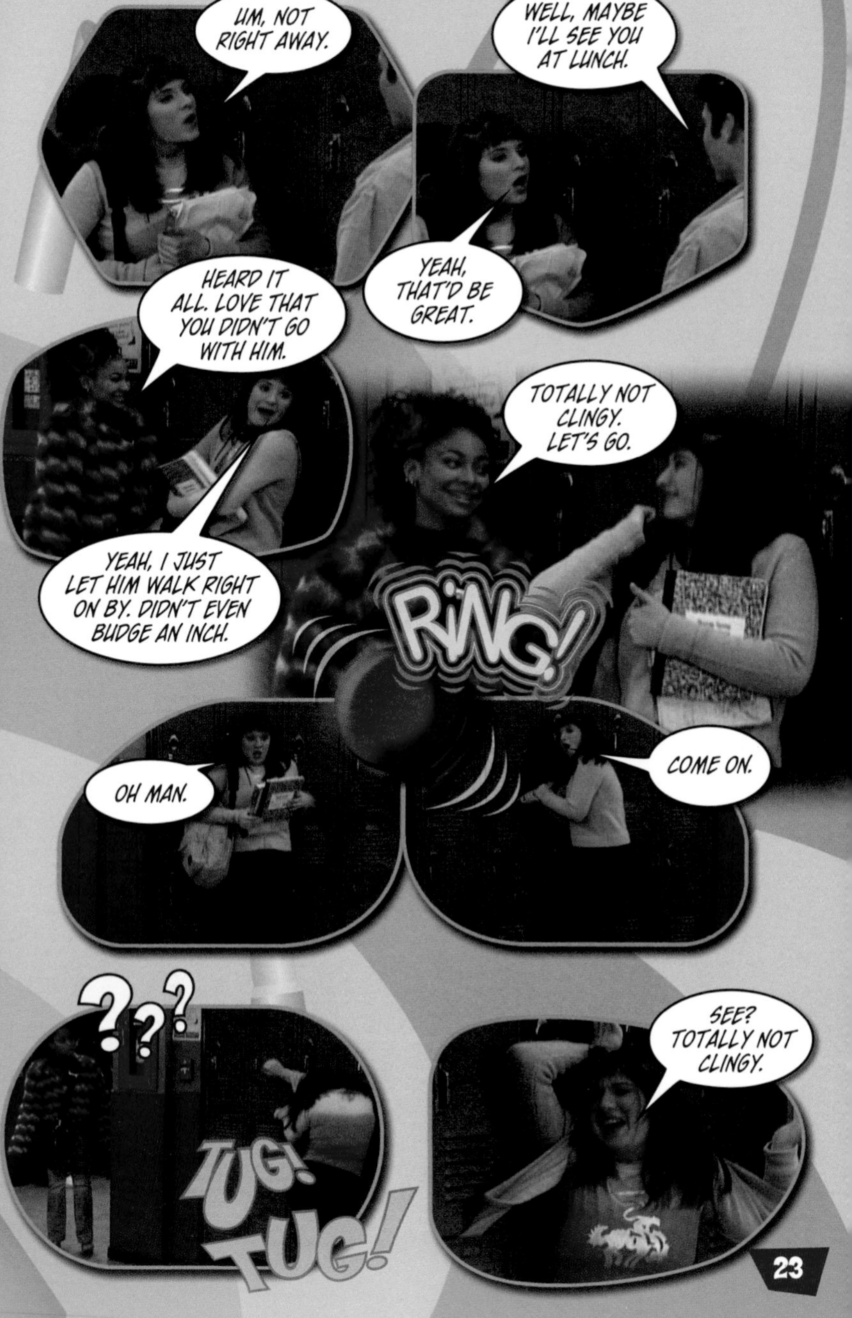
UM, NOT RIGHT AWAY.
WELL, MAYBE I'LL SEE YOU AT LUNCH.
YEAH, THAT'D BE GREAT.
HEARD IT ALL. LOVE THAT YOU DIDN'T GO WITH HIM.
YEAH, I JUST LET HIM WALK RIGHT ON BY. DIDN'T EVEN BUDGE AN INCH.
TOTALLY NOT CLINGY. LET'S GO.
RING!
OH MAN.
COME ON.
???
TUG! TUG!
SEE? TOTALLY NOT CLINGY.

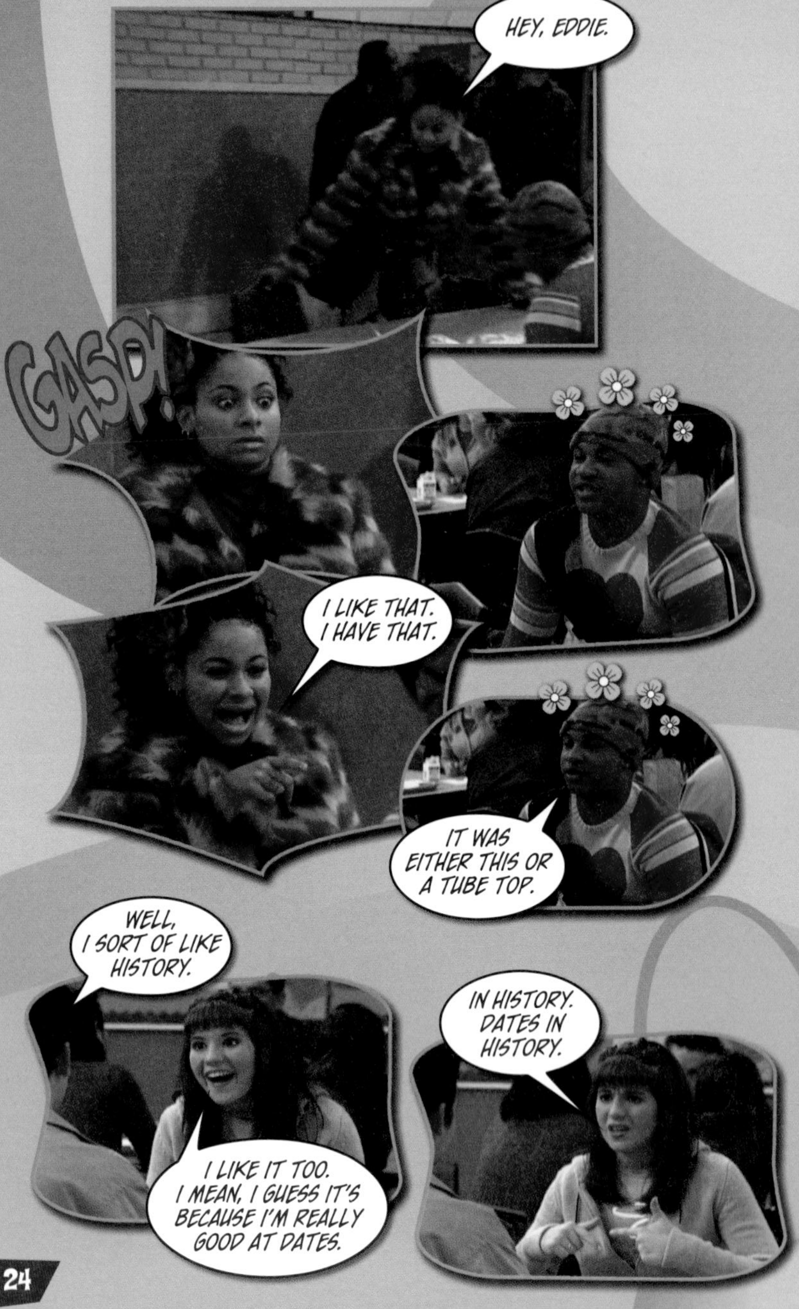
HEY, EDDIE.
GASP!
I LIKE THAT. I HAVE THAT.
IT WAS EITHER THIS OR A TUBE TOP.
WELL, I SORT OF LIKE HISTORY.
I LIKE IT TOO. I MEAN, I GUESS IT'S BECAUSE I'M REALLY GOOD AT DATES.
IN HISTORY. DATES IN HISTORY.

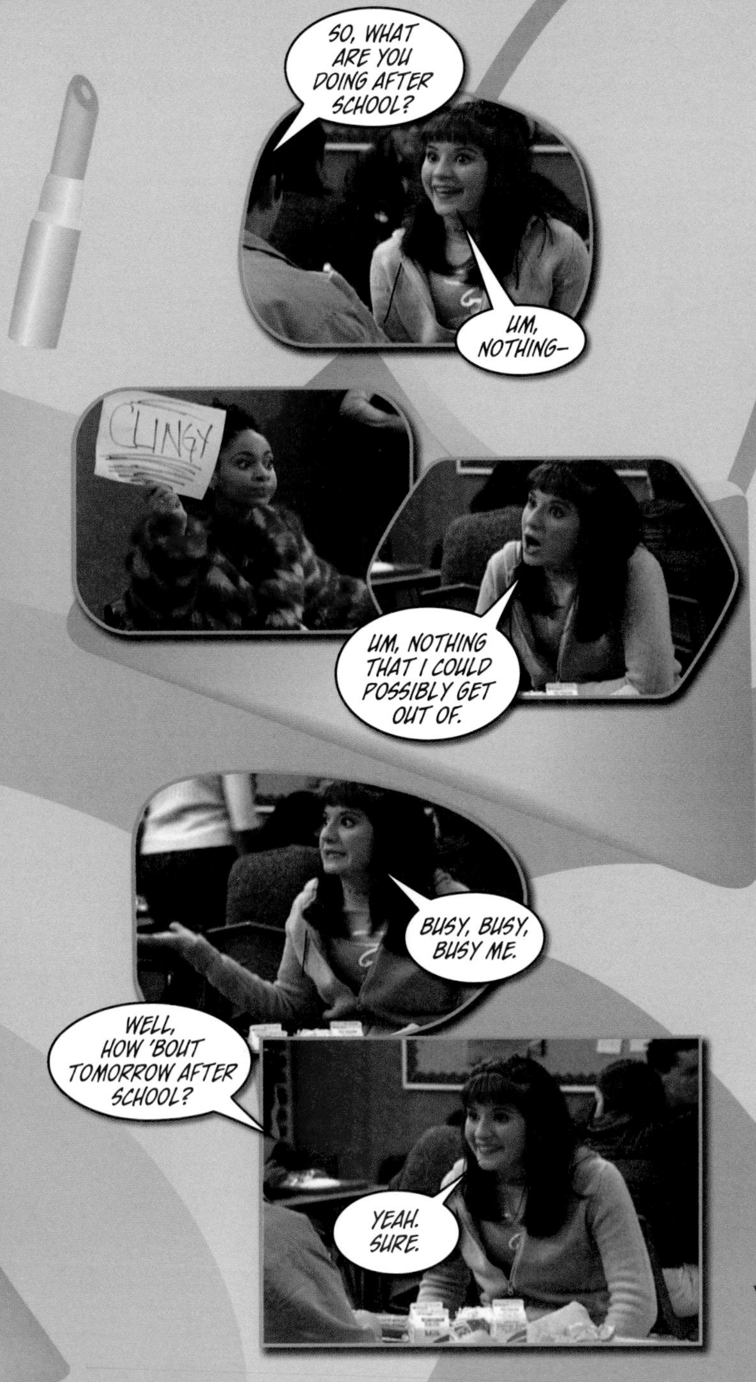
SO, WHAT ARE YOU DOING AFTER SCHOOL?
UM, NOTHING—
CLINGY
UM, NOTHING THAT I COULD POSSIBLY GET OUT OF.
BUSY, BUSY, BUSY ME.
WELL, HOW 'BOUT TOMORROW AFTER SCHOOL?
YEAH. SURE.

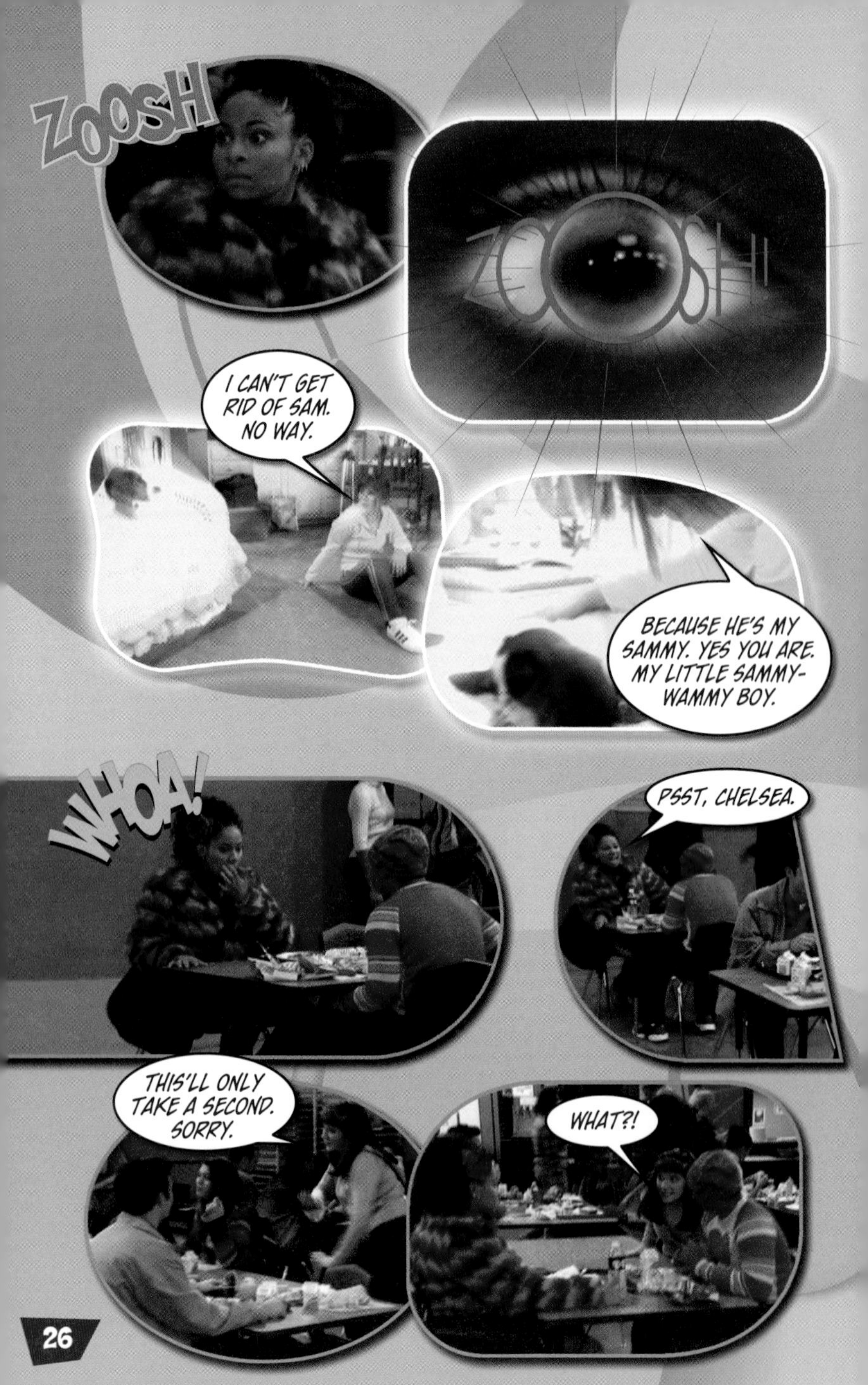
ZOOSH
ZOOSH!
I CAN'T GET RID OF SAM. NO WAY.
BECAUSE HE'S MY SAMMY. YES YOU ARE. MY LITTLE SAMMY-WAMMY BOY.
WHOA!
PSST, CHELSEA.
THIS'LL ONLY TAKE A SECOND. SORRY.
WHAT?!

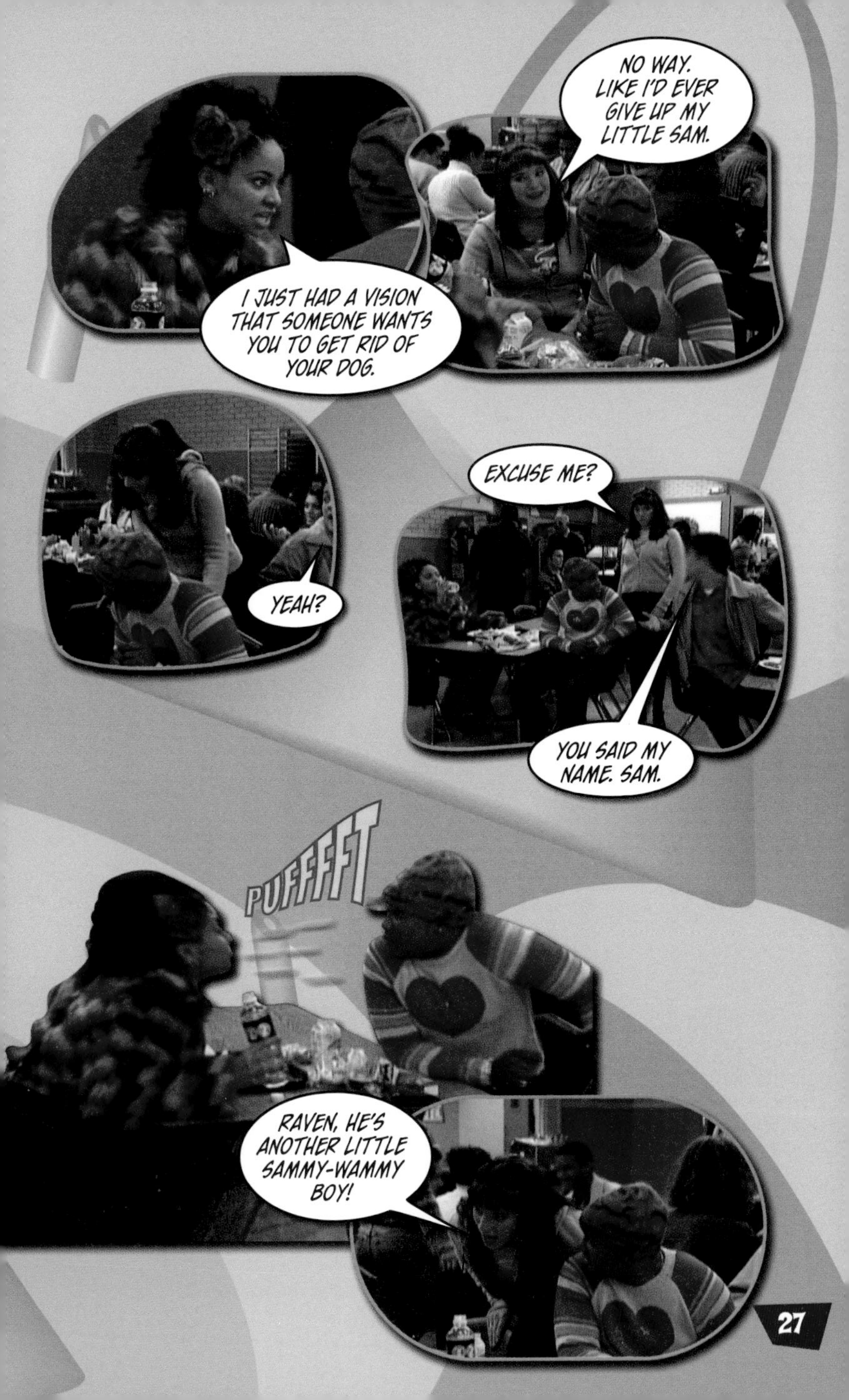
I JUST HAD A VISION THAT SOMEONE WANTS YOU TO GET RID OF YOUR DOG.
NO WAY. LIKE I'D EVER GIVE UP MY LITTLE SAM.
YEAH?
EXCUSE ME?
YOU SAID MY NAME. SAM.
PUFFFFT
RAVEN, HE'S ANOTHER LITTLE SAMMY-WAMMY BOY!

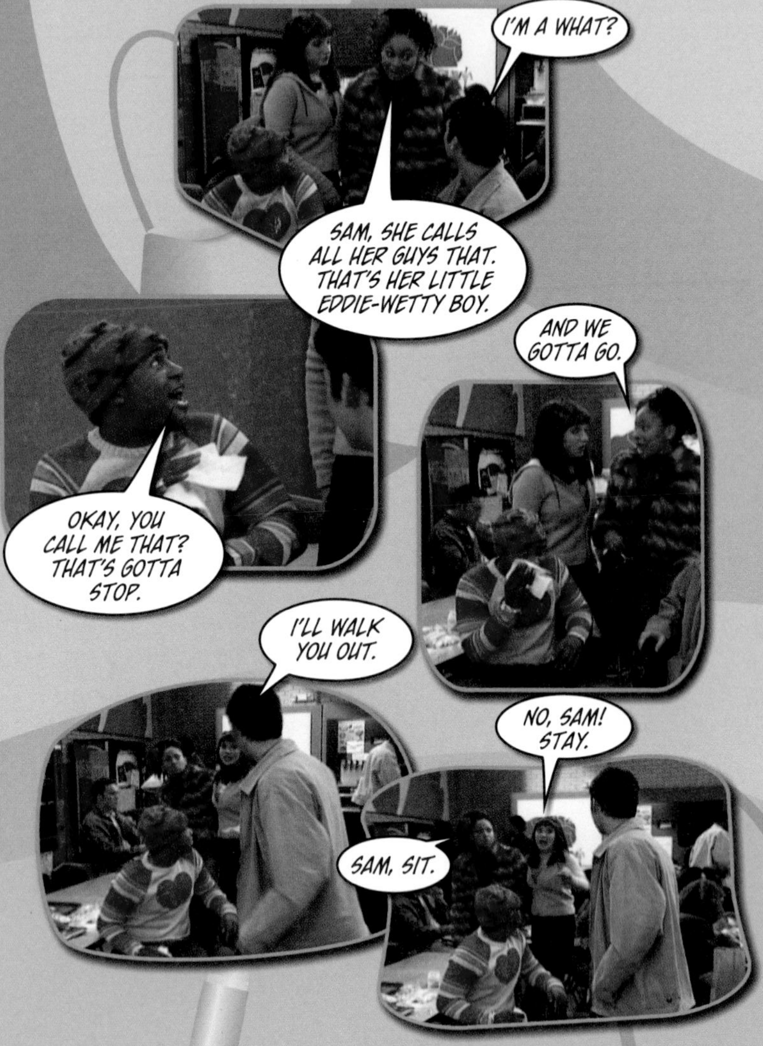
I'M A WHAT?
SAM, SHE CALLS ALL HER GUYS THAT. THAT'S HER LITTLE EDDIE-WETTY BOY.
OKAY, YOU CALL ME THAT? THAT'S GOTTA STOP.
AND WE GOTTA GO.
I'LL WALK YOU OUT.
NO, SAM! STAY.
SAM, SIT.

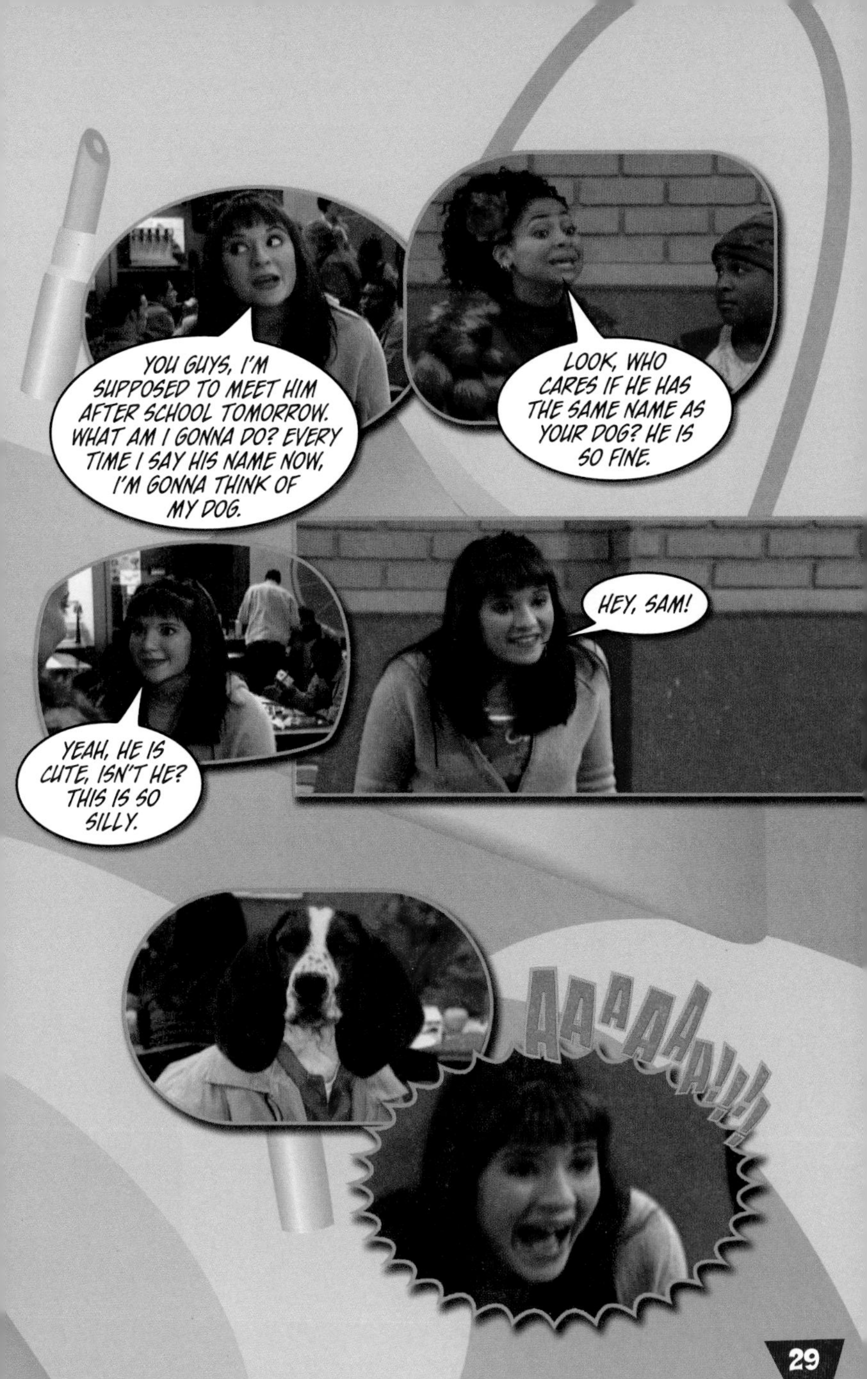
YOU GUYS, I'M SUPPOSED TO MEET HIM AFTER SCHOOL TOMORROW. WHAT AM I GONNA DO? EVERY TIME I SAY HIS NAME NOW, I'M GONNA THINK OF MY DOG.
LOOK, WHO CARES IF HE HAS THE SAME NAME AS YOUR DOG? HE IS SO FINE.
YEAH, HE IS CUTE, ISN'T HE? THIS IS SO SILLY.
HEY, SAM!
AAAAAAH!!!

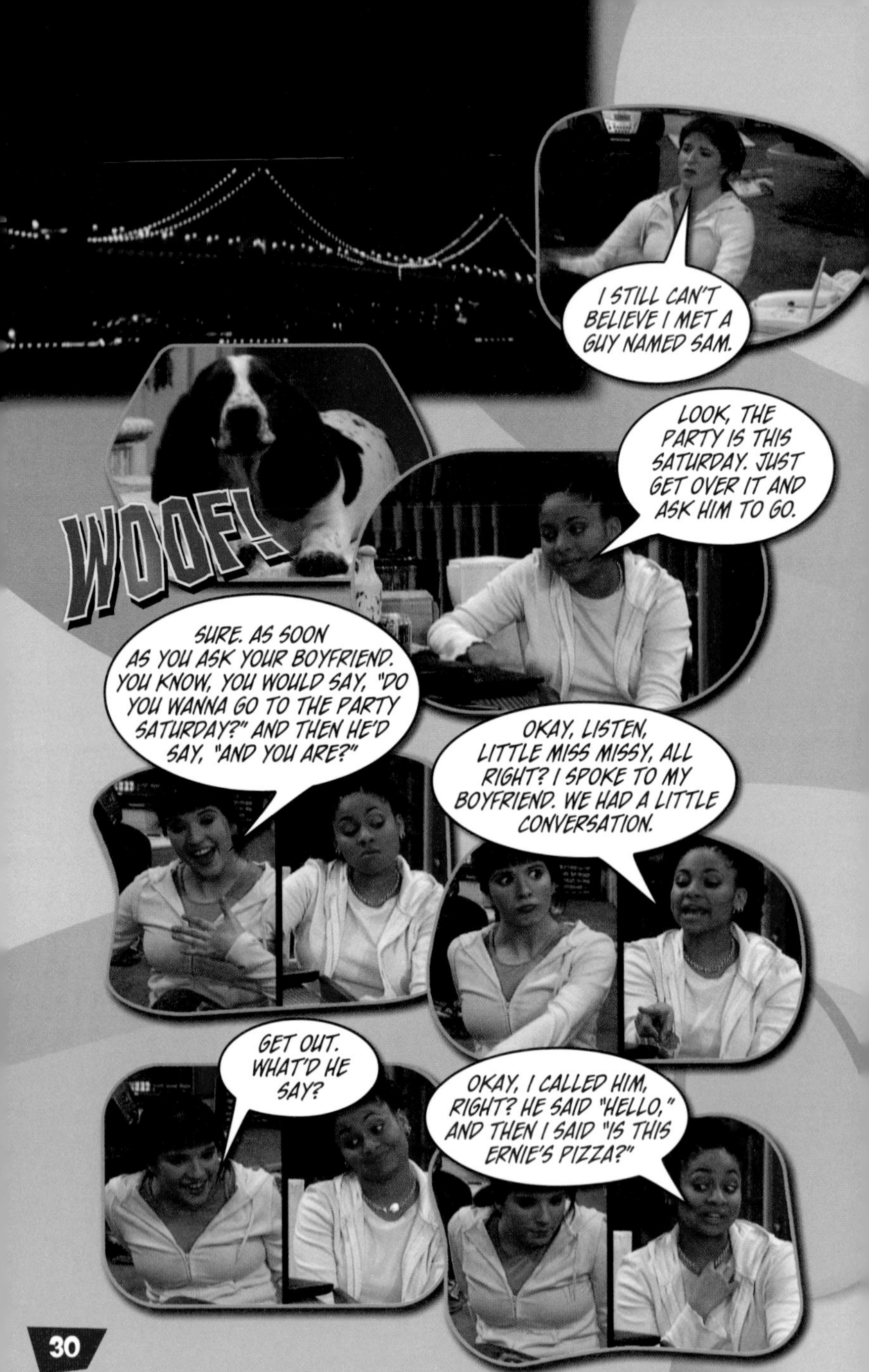
I STILL CAN'T BELIEVE I MET A GUY NAMED SAM.
WOOF!
LOOK, THE PARTY IS THIS SATURDAY. JUST GET OVER IT AND ASK HIM TO GO.
SURE. AS SOON AS YOU ASK YOUR BOYFRIEND. YOU KNOW, YOU WOULD SAY, "DO YOU WANNA GO TO THE PARTY SATURDAY?" AND THEN HE'D SAY, "AND YOU ARE?"
OKAY, LISTEN, LITTLE MISS MISSY, ALL RIGHT? I SPOKE TO MY BOYFRIEND. WE HAD A LITTLE CONVERSATION.
GET OUT. WHAT'D HE SAY?
OKAY, I CALLED HIM, RIGHT? HE SAID "HELLO," AND THEN I SAID "IS THIS ERNIE'S PIZZA?"

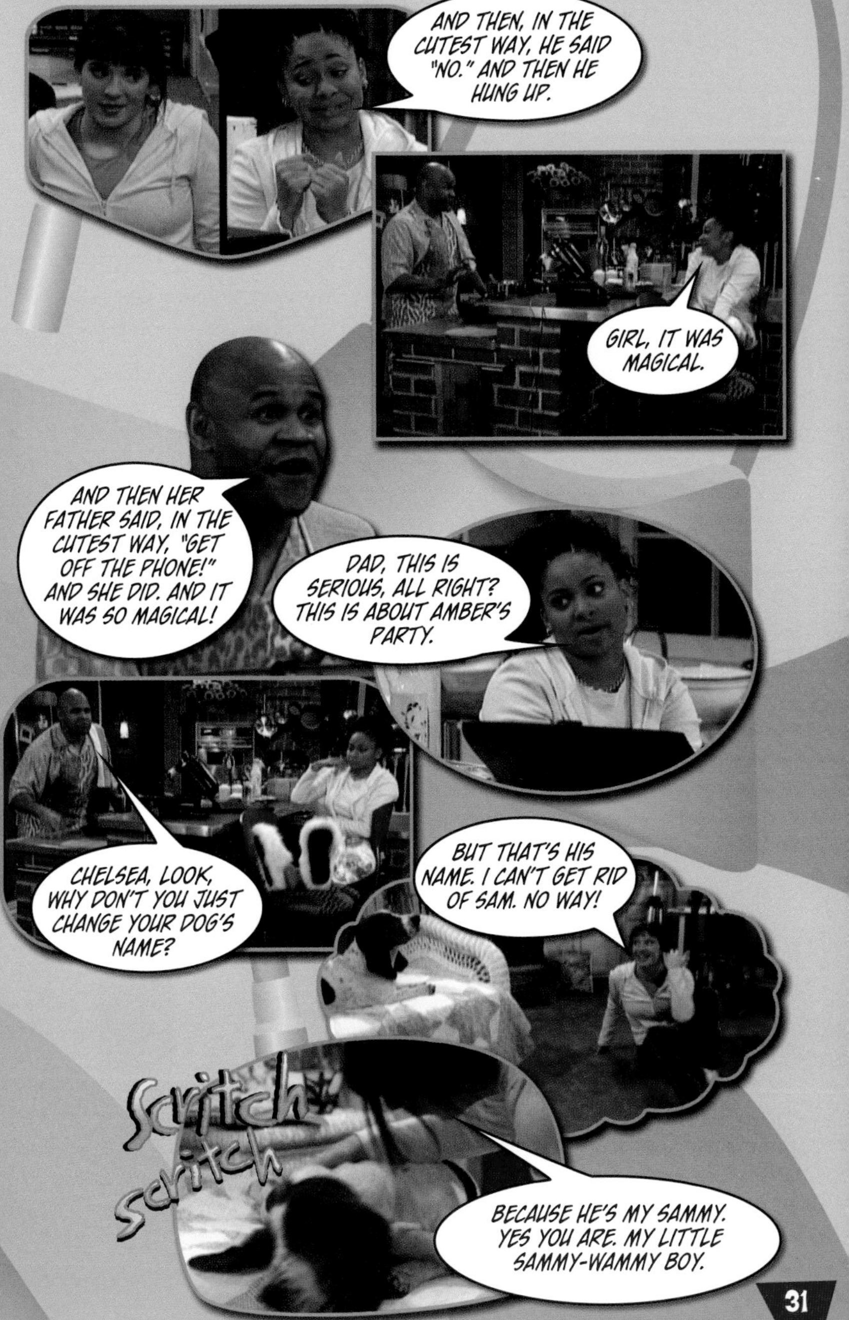
AND THEN, IN THE CUTEST WAY, HE SAID "NO." AND THEN HE HUNG UP.
GIRL, IT WAS MAGICAL.
AND THEN HER FATHER SAID, IN THE CUTEST WAY, "GET OFF THE PHONE!" AND SHE DID. AND IT WAS SO MAGICAL!
DAD, THIS IS SERIOUS, ALL RIGHT? THIS IS ABOUT AMBER'S PARTY.
CHELSEA, LOOK, WHY DON'T YOU JUST CHANGE YOUR DOG'S NAME?
BUT THAT'S HIS NAME. I CAN'T GET RID OF SAM. NO WAY!
Scritch scritch
BECAUSE HE'S MY SAMMY. YES YOU ARE. MY LITTLE SAMMY-WAMMY BOY.

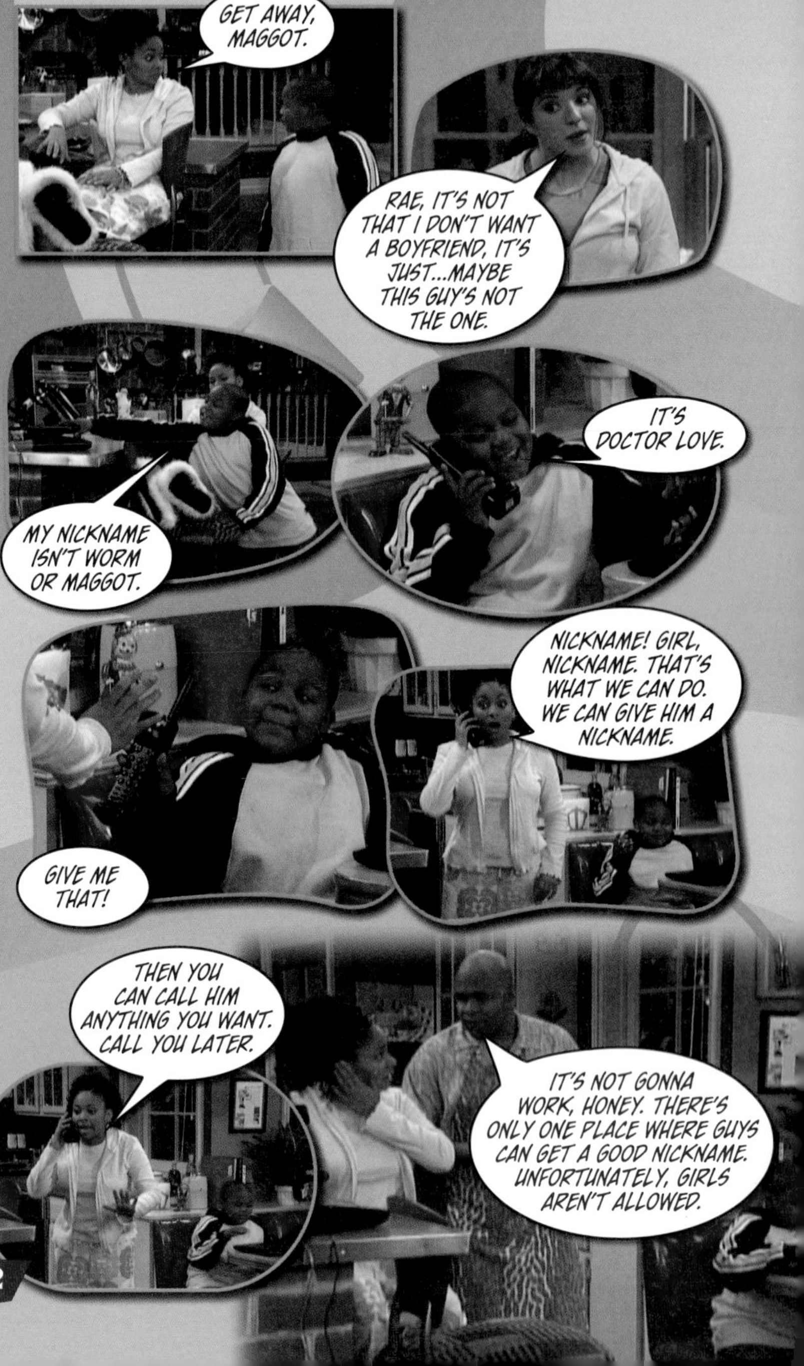
GET AWAY, MAGGOT.
RAE, IT'S NOT THAT I DON'T WANT A BOYFRIEND, IT'S JUST...MAYBE THIS GUY'S NOT THE ONE.
MY NICKNAME ISN'T WORM OR MAGGOT.
IT'S DOCTOR LOVE.
GIVE ME THAT!
NICKNAME! GIRL, NICKNAME. THAT'S WHAT WE CAN DO. WE CAN GIVE HIM A NICKNAME.
THEN YOU CAN CALL HIM ANYTHING YOU WANT. CALL YOU LATER.
IT'S NOT GONNA WORK, HONEY. THERE'S ONLY ONE PLACE WHERE GUYS CAN GET A GOOD NICKNAME. UNFORTUNATELY, GIRLS AREN'T ALLOWED.

WHERE?
AH-HA! TELL HER, SON.
ARRRRGGGGHHHH!!!
THE GYM!
NEXT DAY
GET OUT HERE!

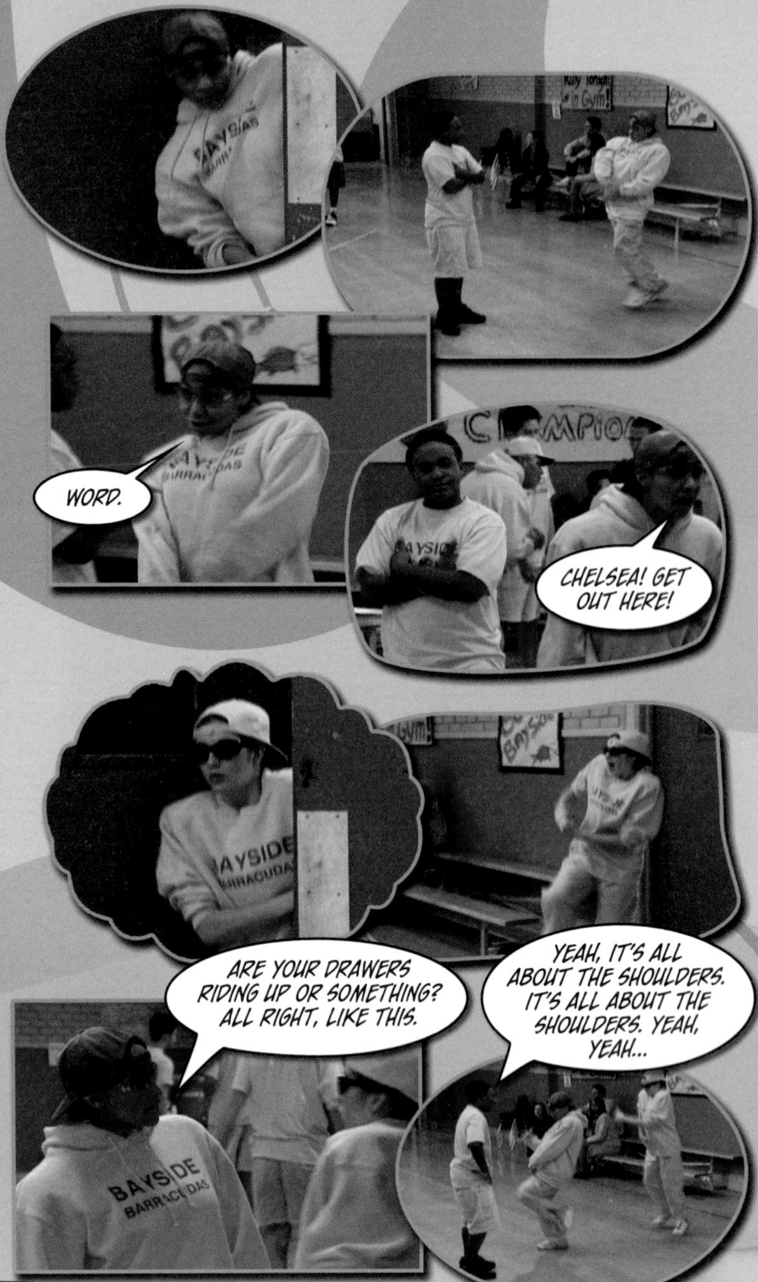
WORD.
CHELSEA! GET OUT HERE!
ARE YOUR DRAWERS RIDING UP OR SOMETHING? ALL RIGHT, LIKE THIS.
YEAH, IT'S ALL ABOUT THE SHOULDERS. IT'S ALL ABOUT THE SHOULDERS. YEAH, YEAH...

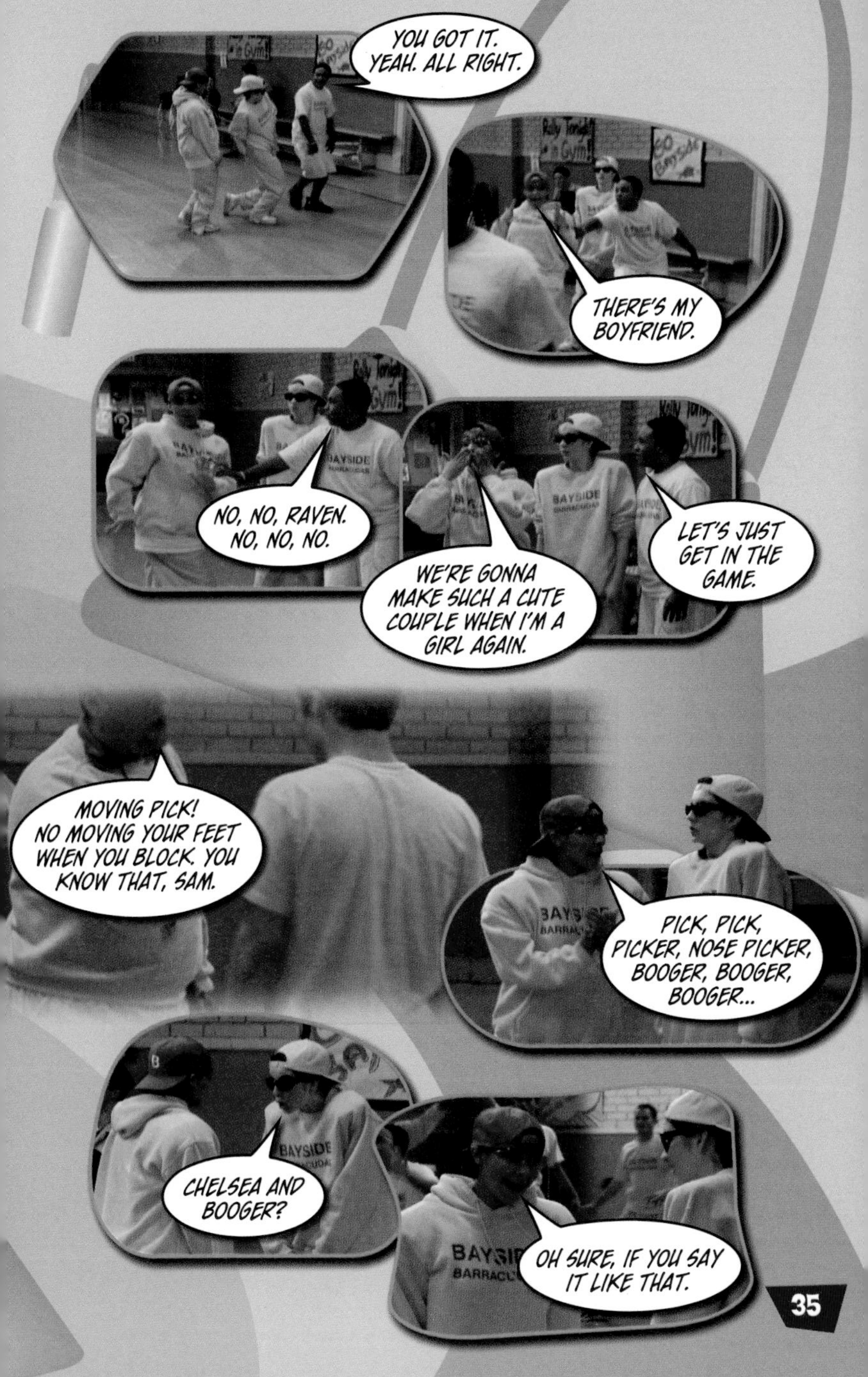

YOU GOT IT. YEAH. ALL RIGHT.
THERE'S MY BOYFRIEND.
NO, NO, RAVEN. NO, NO, NO.
WE'RE GONNA MAKE SUCH A CUTE COUPLE WHEN I'M A GIRL AGAIN.
LET'S JUST GET IN THE GAME.
MOVING PICK! NO MOVING YOUR FEET WHEN YOU BLOCK. YOU KNOW THAT, SAM.
PICK, PICK, PICKER, NOSE PICKER, BOOGER, BOOGER, BOOGER...
CHELSEA AND BOOGER?
OH SURE, IF YOU SAY IT LIKE THAT.

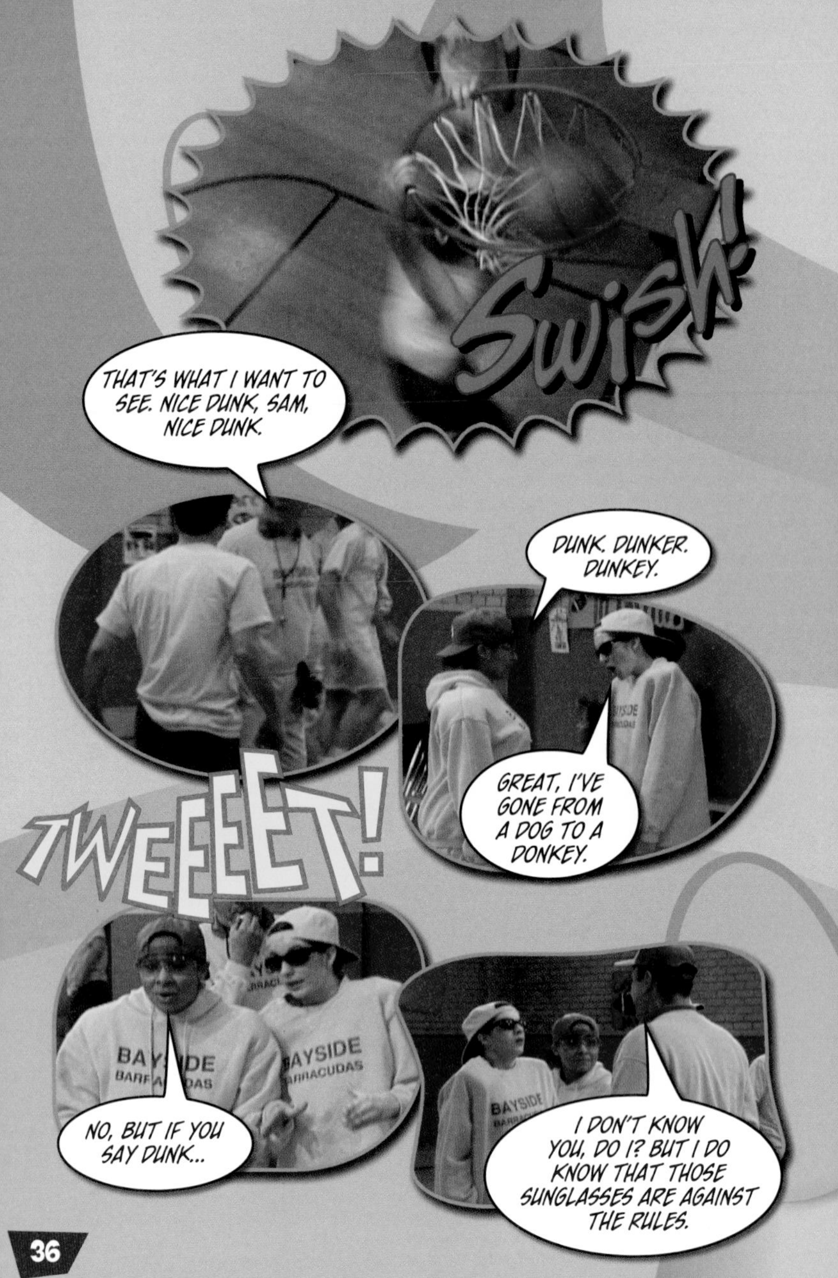
SWISH!
THAT'S WHAT I WANT TO SEE. NICE DUNK, SAM, NICE DUNK.
DUNK. DUNKER. DUNKEY.
GREAT, I'VE GONE FROM A DOG TO A DONKEY.
TWEEEET!
BAYSIDE BARRACUDAS
NO, BUT IF YOU SAY DUNK...
I DON'T KNOW YOU, DO I? BUT I DO KNOW THAT THOSE SUNGLASSES ARE AGAINST THE RULES.

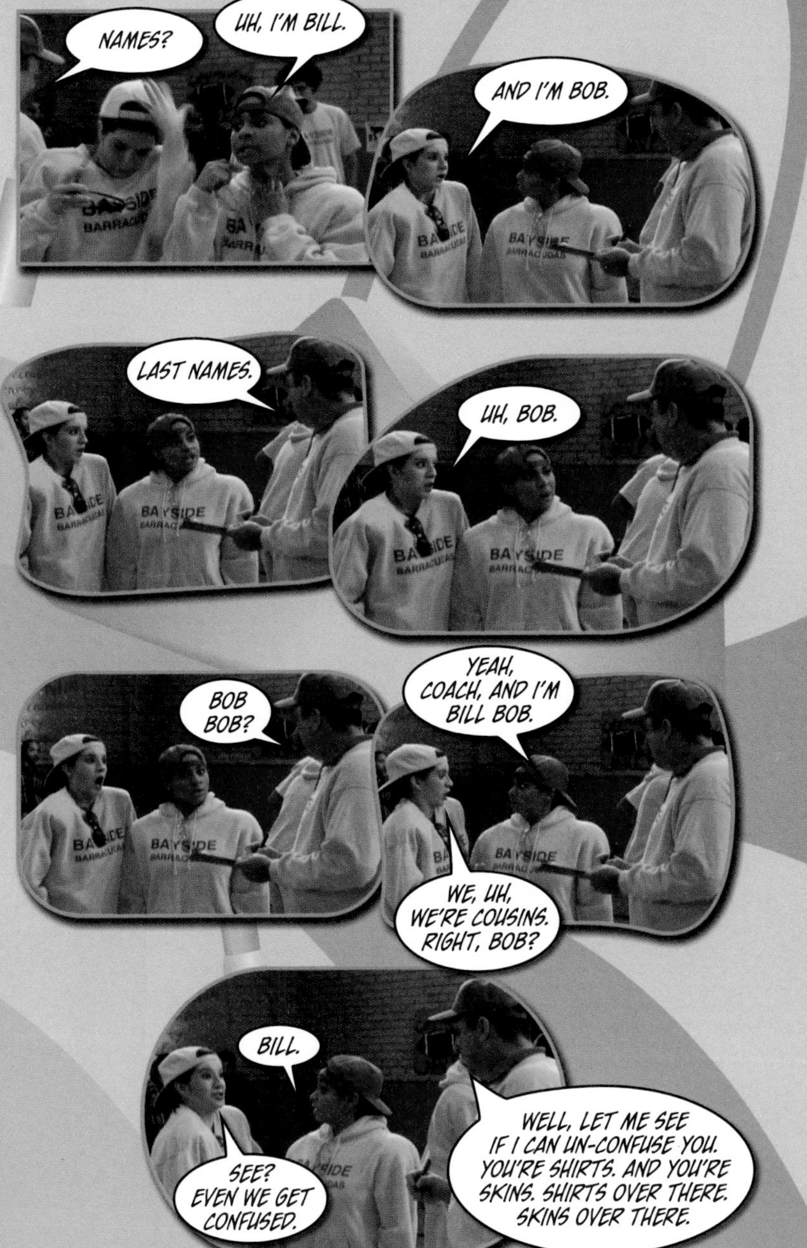
NAMES?
UH, I'M BILL.
AND I'M BOB.
LAST NAMES.
UH, BOB.
BOB BOB?
YEAH, COACH, AND I'M BILL BOB.
WE, UH, WE'RE COUSINS. RIGHT, BOB?
BILL.
SEE? EVEN WE GET CONFUSED.
WELL, LET ME SEE IF I CAN UN-CONFUSE YOU. YOU'RE SHIRTS. AND YOU'RE SKINS. SHIRTS OVER THERE. SKINS OVER THERE.

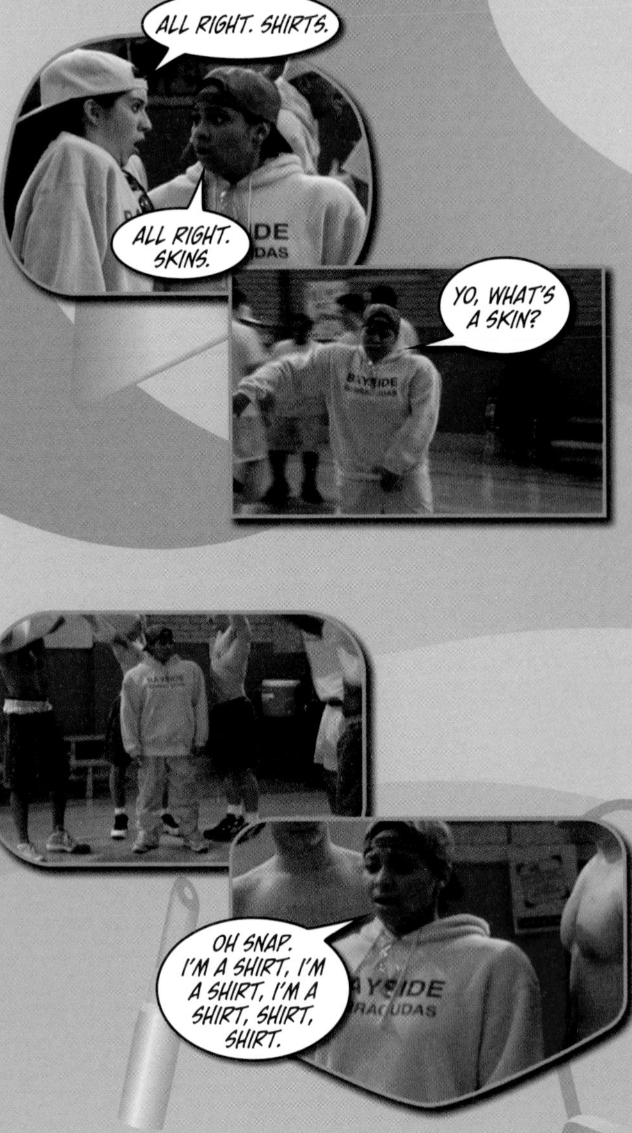
ALL RIGHT. SHIRTS.
ALL RIGHT. SKINS.
YO, WHAT'S A SKIN?
OH SNAP. I'M A SHIRT, I'M A SHIRT, I'M A SHIRT, SHIRT, SHIRT.

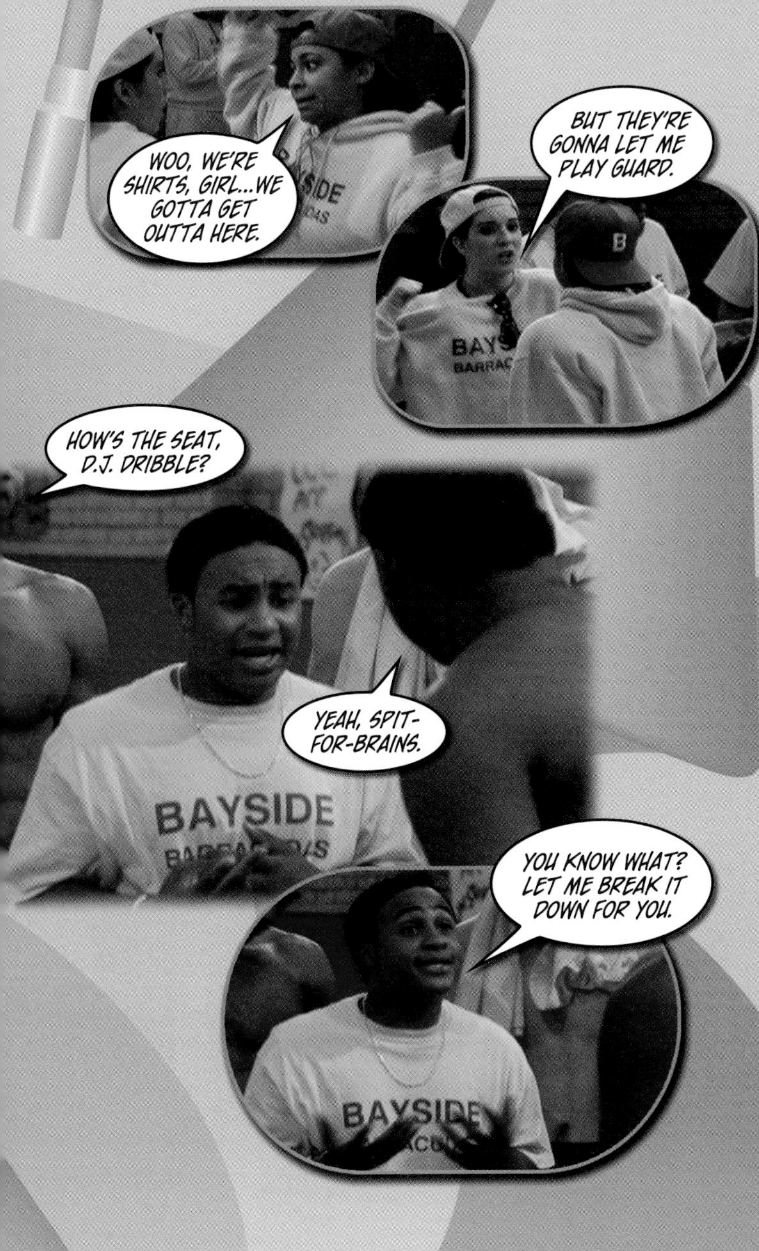
WOO, WE'RE SHIRTS, GIRL...WE GOTTA GET OUTTA HERE.
BUT THEY'RE GONNA LET ME PLAY GUARD.
HOW'S THE SEAT, D.J. DRIBBLE?
YEAH, SPIT-FOR-BRAINS.
YOU KNOW WHAT? LET ME BREAK IT DOWN FOR YOU.

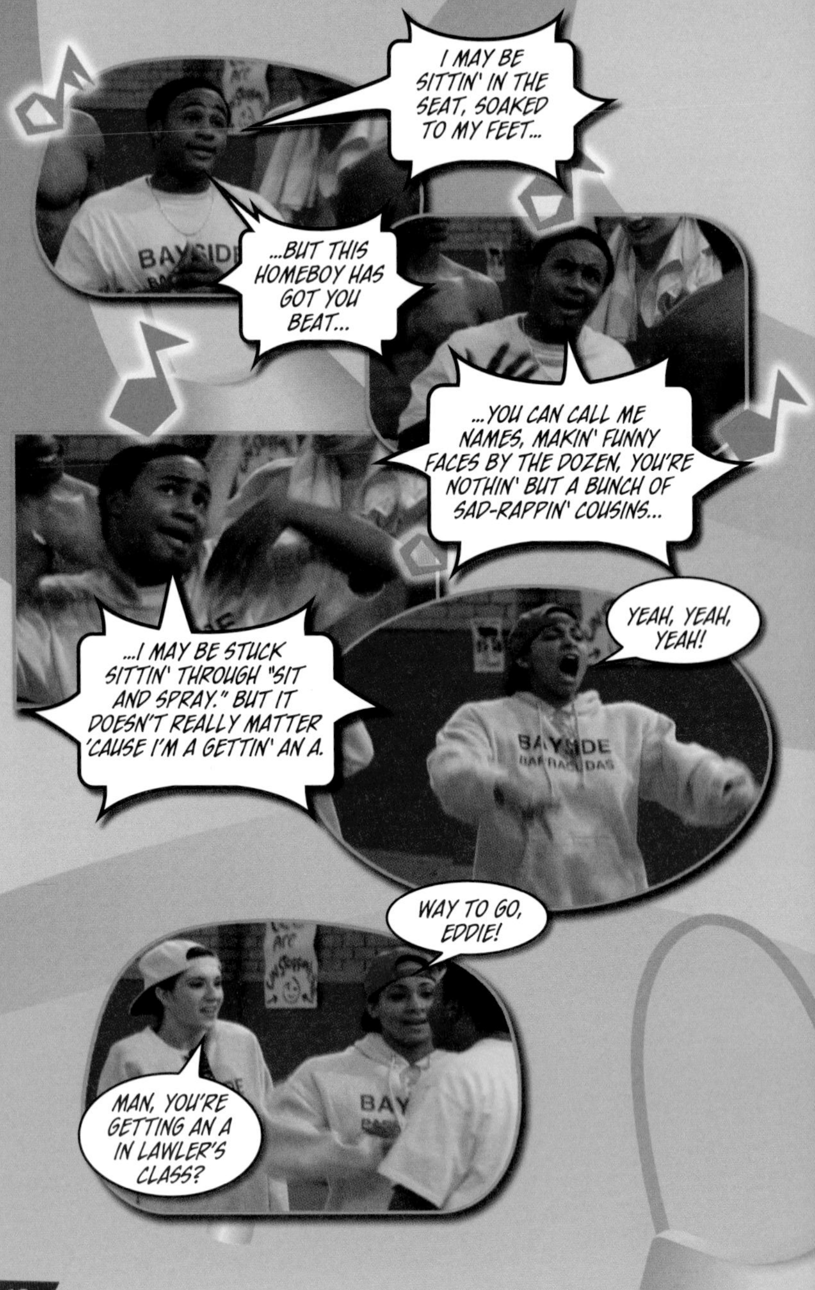
I MAY BE SITTIN' IN THE SEAT, SOAKED TO MY FEET...
...BUT THIS HOMEBOY HAS GOT YOU BEAT...
...YOU CAN CALL ME NAMES, MAKIN' FUNNY FACES BY THE DOZEN, YOU'RE NOTHIN' BUT A BUNCH OF SAD-RAPPIN' COUSINS...
...I MAY BE STUCK SITTIN' THROUGH "SIT AND SPRAY." BUT IT DOESN'T REALLY MATTER 'CAUSE I'M A GETTIN' AN A.
YEAH, YEAH, YEAH!
WAY TO GO, EDDIE!
MAN, YOU'RE GETTING AN A IN LAWLER'S CLASS?

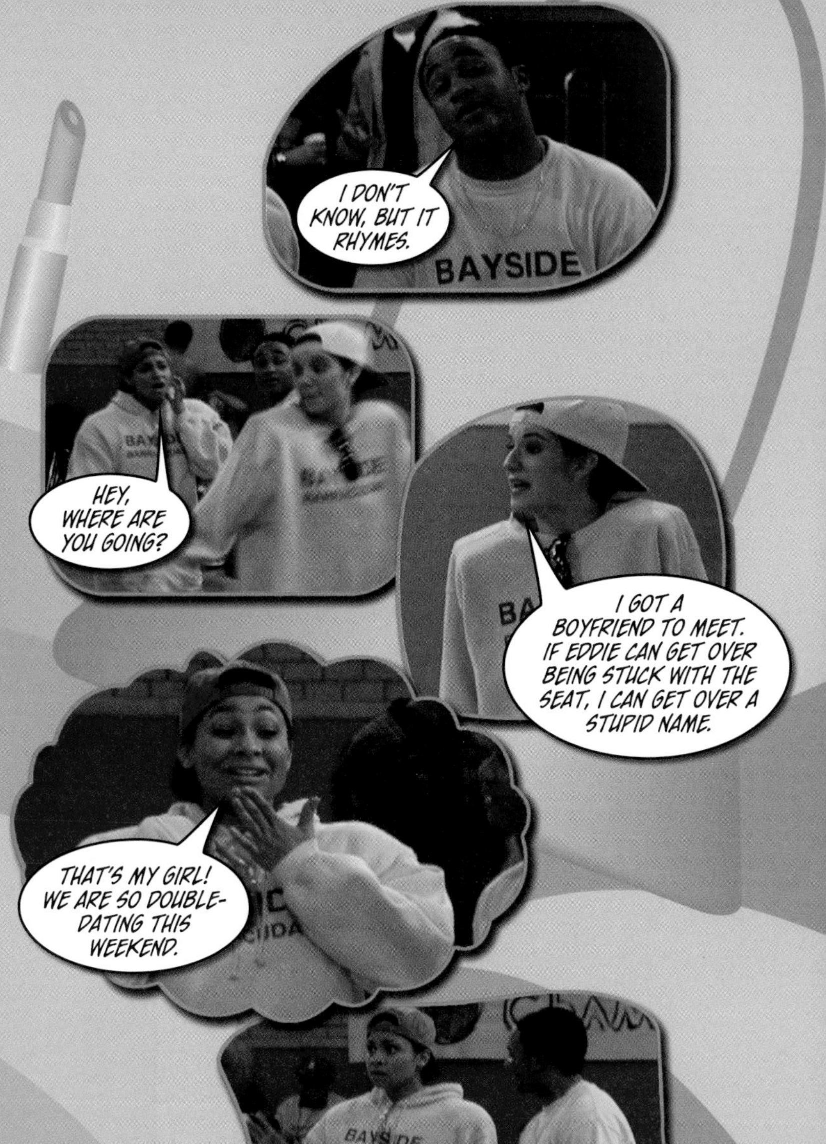
I DON'T KNOW, BUT IT RHYMES.
BAYSIDE
HEY, WHERE ARE YOU GOING?
I GOT A BOYFRIEND TO MEET. IF EDDIE CAN GET OVER BEING STUCK WITH THE SEAT, I CAN GET OVER A STUPID NAME.
THAT'S MY GIRL! WE ARE SO DOUBLE-DATING THIS WEEKEND.
BAYSIDE

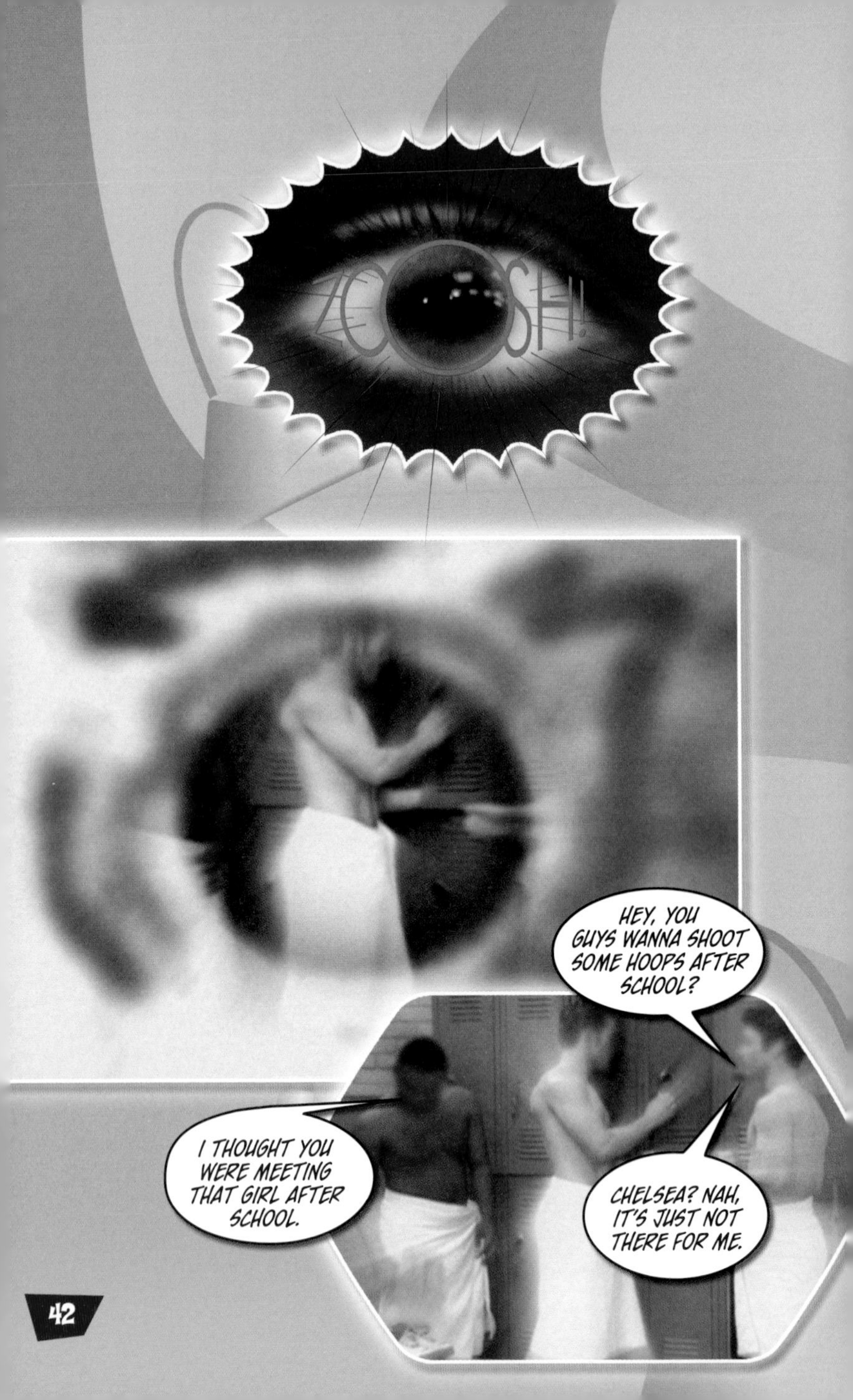
ZOOSH!
HEY, YOU GUYS WANNA SHOOT SOME HOOPS AFTER SCHOOL?
I THOUGHT YOU WERE MEETING THAT GIRL AFTER SCHOOL.
CHELSEA? NAH, IT'S JUST NOT THERE FOR ME.

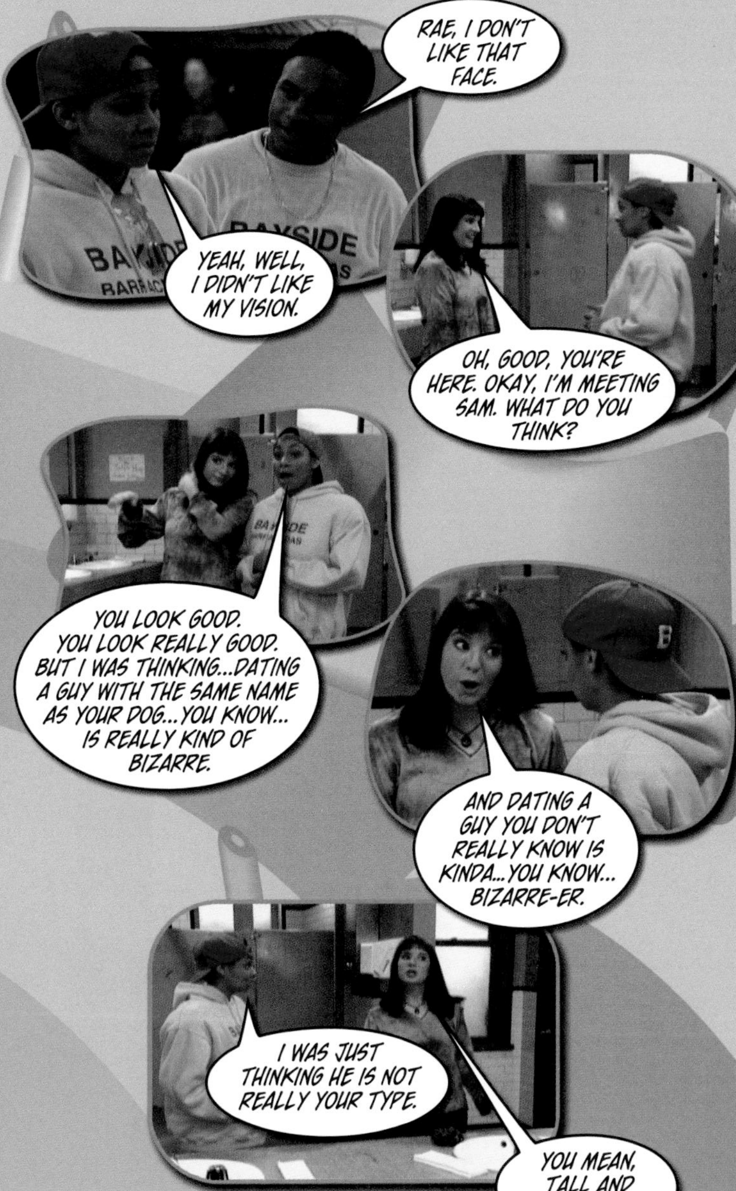

RAE, I DON'T LIKE THAT FACE.
YEAH, WELL, I DIDN'T LIKE MY VISION.
OH, GOOD, YOU'RE HERE. OKAY, I'M MEETING SAM. WHAT DO YOU THINK?
YOU LOOK GOOD. YOU LOOK REALLY GOOD. BUT I WAS THINKING...DATING A GUY WITH THE SAME NAME AS YOUR DOG...YOU KNOW... IS REALLY KIND OF BIZARRE.
AND DATING A GUY YOU DON'T REALLY KNOW IS KINDA...YOU KNOW... BIZARRE-ER.
I WAS JUST THINKING HE IS NOT REALLY YOUR TYPE.
YOU MEAN, TALL AND REALLY CUTE?

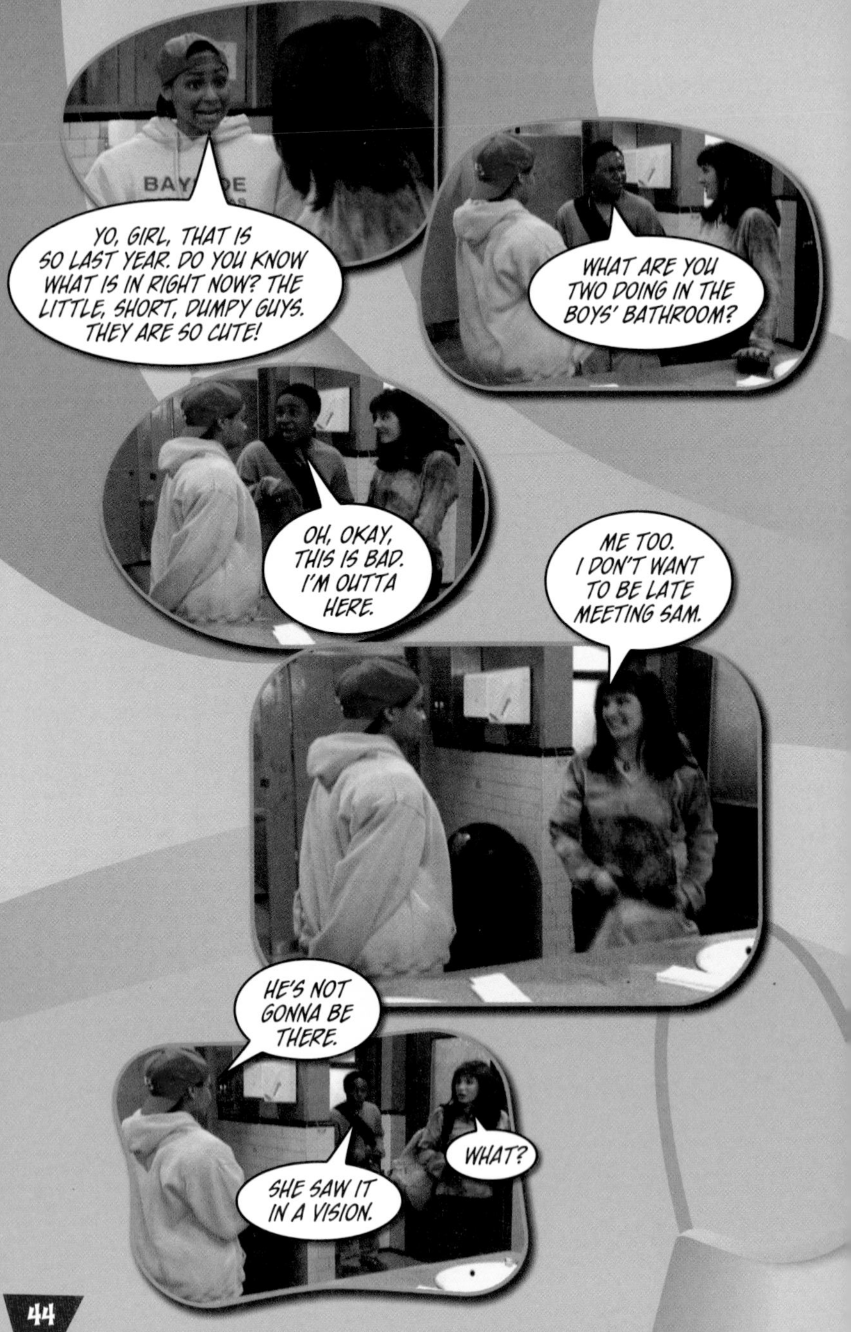
YO, GIRL, THAT IS SO LAST YEAR. DO YOU KNOW WHAT IS IN RIGHT NOW? THE LITTLE, SHORT, DUMPY GUYS. THEY ARE SO CUTE!
WHAT ARE YOU TWO DOING IN THE BOYS' BATHROOM?
OH, OKAY, THIS IS BAD. I'M OUTTA HERE.
ME TOO. I DON'T WANT TO BE LATE MEETING SAM.
HE'S NOT GONNA BE THERE.
WHAT?
SHE SAW IT IN A VISION.

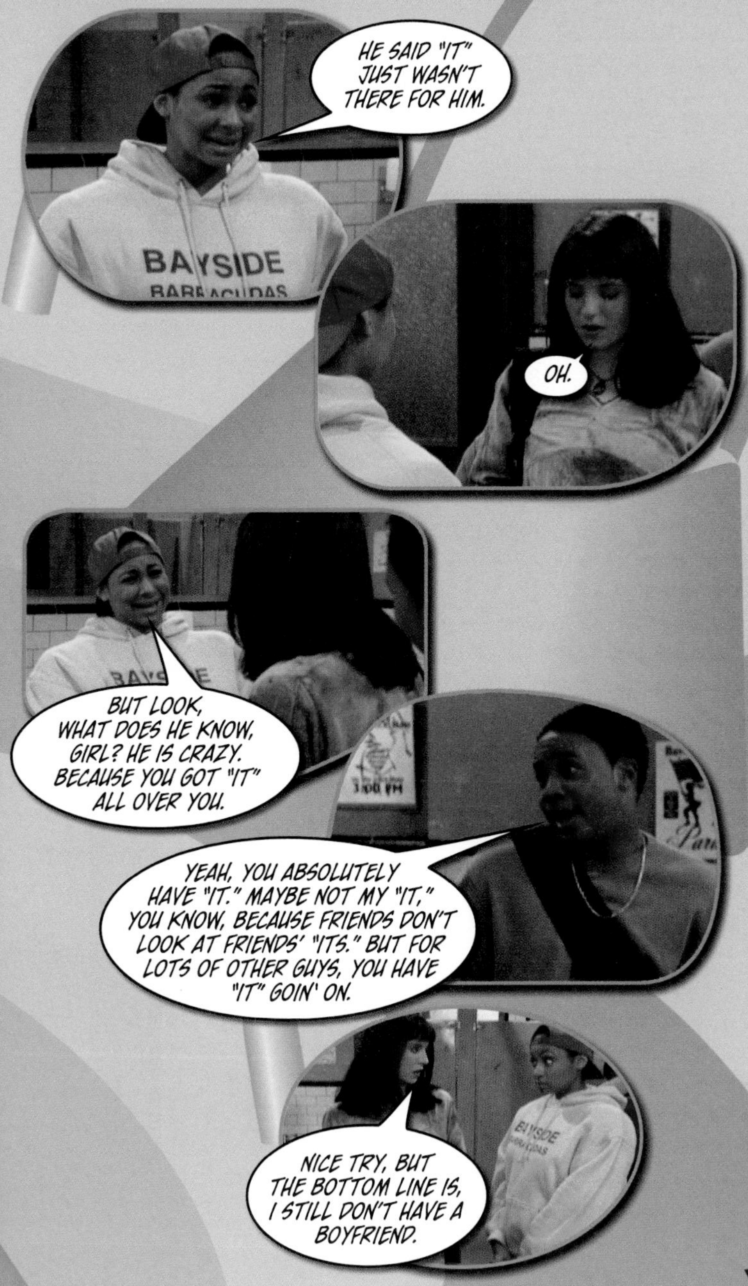
HE SAID "IT" JUST WASN'T THERE FOR HIM.
BAYSIDE BARRACUDAS
OH.
BUT LOOK, WHAT DOES HE KNOW, GIRL? HE IS CRAZY. BECAUSE YOU GOT "IT" ALL OVER YOU.
YEAH, YOU ABSOLUTELY HAVE "IT." MAYBE NOT MY "IT," YOU KNOW, BECAUSE FRIENDS DON'T LOOK AT FRIENDS' "ITS." BUT FOR LOTS OF OTHER GUYS, YOU HAVE "IT" GOIN' ON.
NICE TRY, BUT THE BOTTOM LINE IS, I STILL DON'T HAVE A BOYFRIEND.

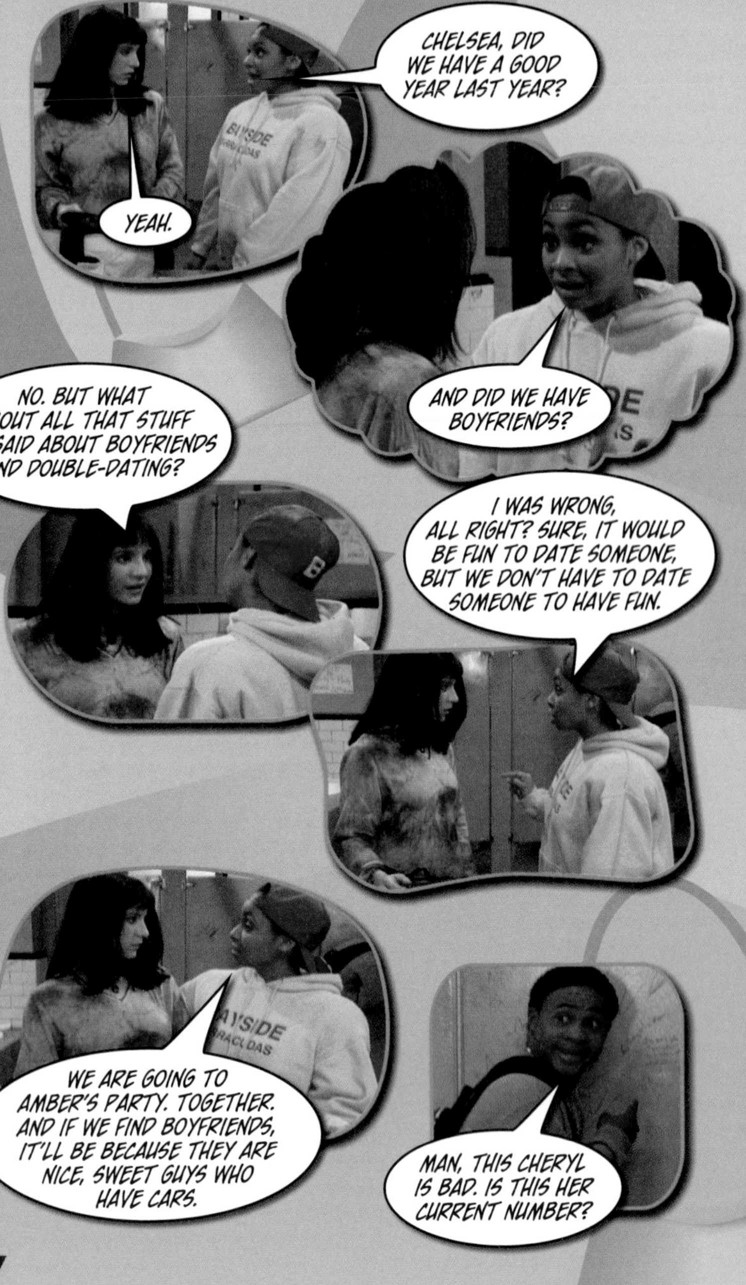
CHELSEA, DID WE HAVE A GOOD YEAR LAST YEAR?
YEAH.
AND DID WE HAVE BOYFRIENDS?
NO. BUT WHAT ABOUT ALL THAT STUFF YOU SAID ABOUT BOYFRIENDS AND DOUBLE-DATING?
I WAS WRONG, ALL RIGHT? SURE, IT WOULD BE FUN TO DATE SOMEONE, BUT WE DON'T HAVE TO DATE SOMEONE TO HAVE FUN.
WE ARE GOING TO AMBER'S PARTY. TOGETHER. AND IF WE FIND BOYFRIENDS, IT'LL BE BECAUSE THEY ARE NICE, SWEET GUYS WHO HAVE CARS.
MAN, THIS CHERYL IS BAD. IS THIS HER CURRENT NUMBER?

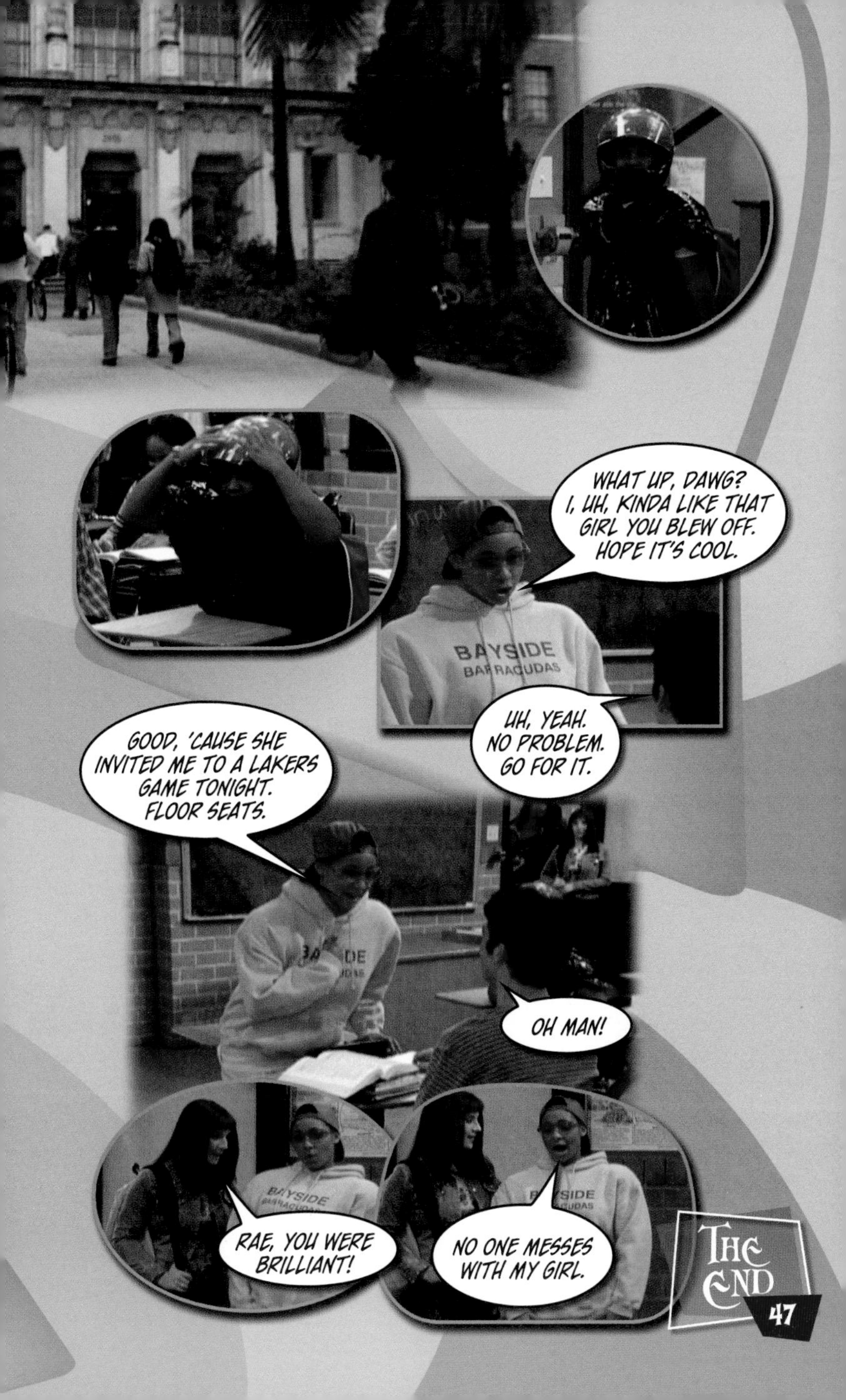
WHAT UP, DAWG? I, UH, KINDA LIKE THAT GIRL YOU BLEW OFF. HOPE IT'S COOL.
UH, YEAH. NO PROBLEM. GO FOR IT.
GOOD, 'CAUSE SHE INVITED ME TO A LAKERS GAME TONIGHT. FLOOR SEATS.
OH MAN!
RAE, YOU WERE BRILLIANT!
NO ONE MESSES WITH MY GIRL.
THE END

DRIVEN TO INSANITY

WRITTEN BY
DAVA SAVAL

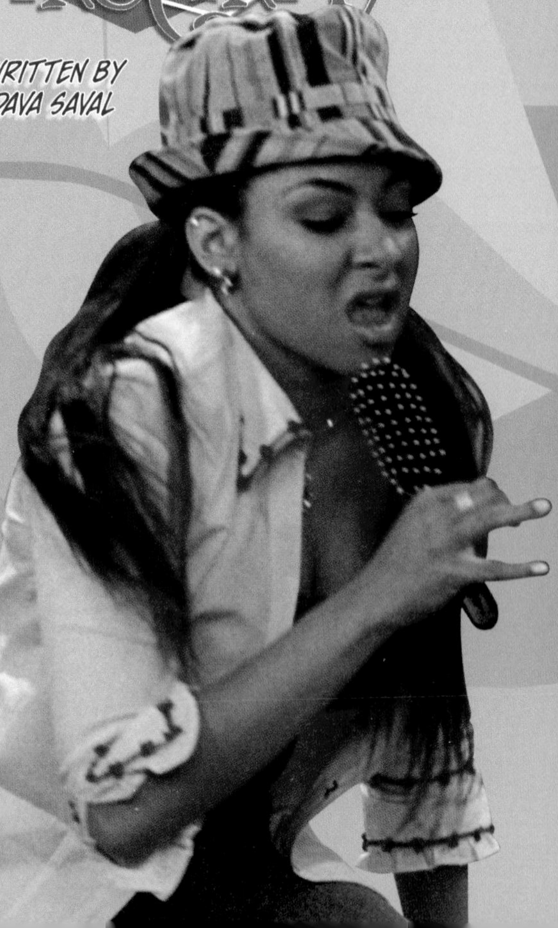

that's so raven

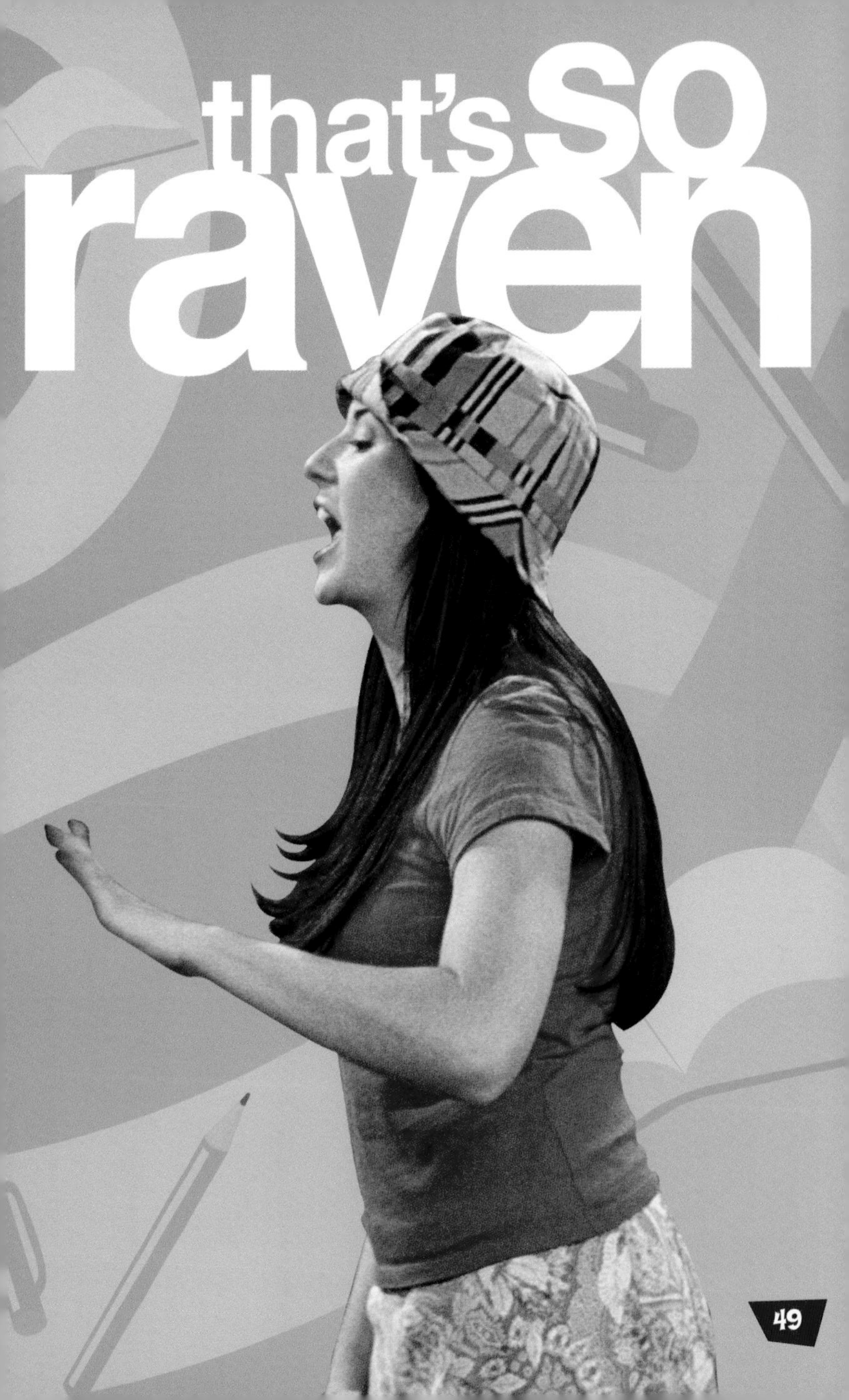

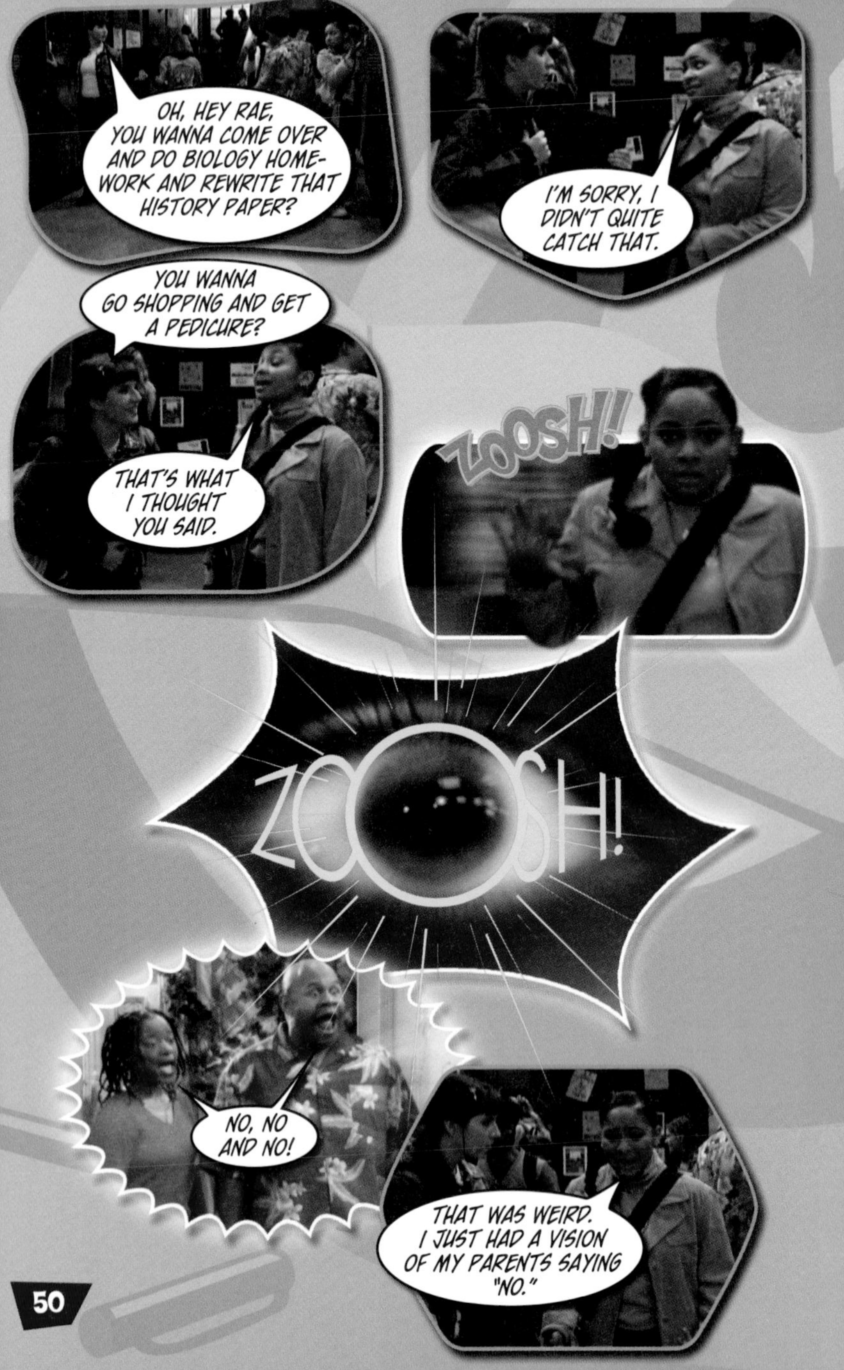
OH, HEY RAE, YOU WANNA COME OVER AND DO BIOLOGY HOME-WORK AND REWRITE THAT HISTORY PAPER?
I'M SORRY, I DIDN'T QUITE CATCH THAT.
YOU WANNA GO SHOPPING AND GET A PEDICURE?
THAT'S WHAT I THOUGHT YOU SAID.
ZOOSH!
ZOOSH!
NO, NO AND NO!
THAT WAS WEIRD. I JUST HAD A VISION OF MY PARENTS SAYING "NO."

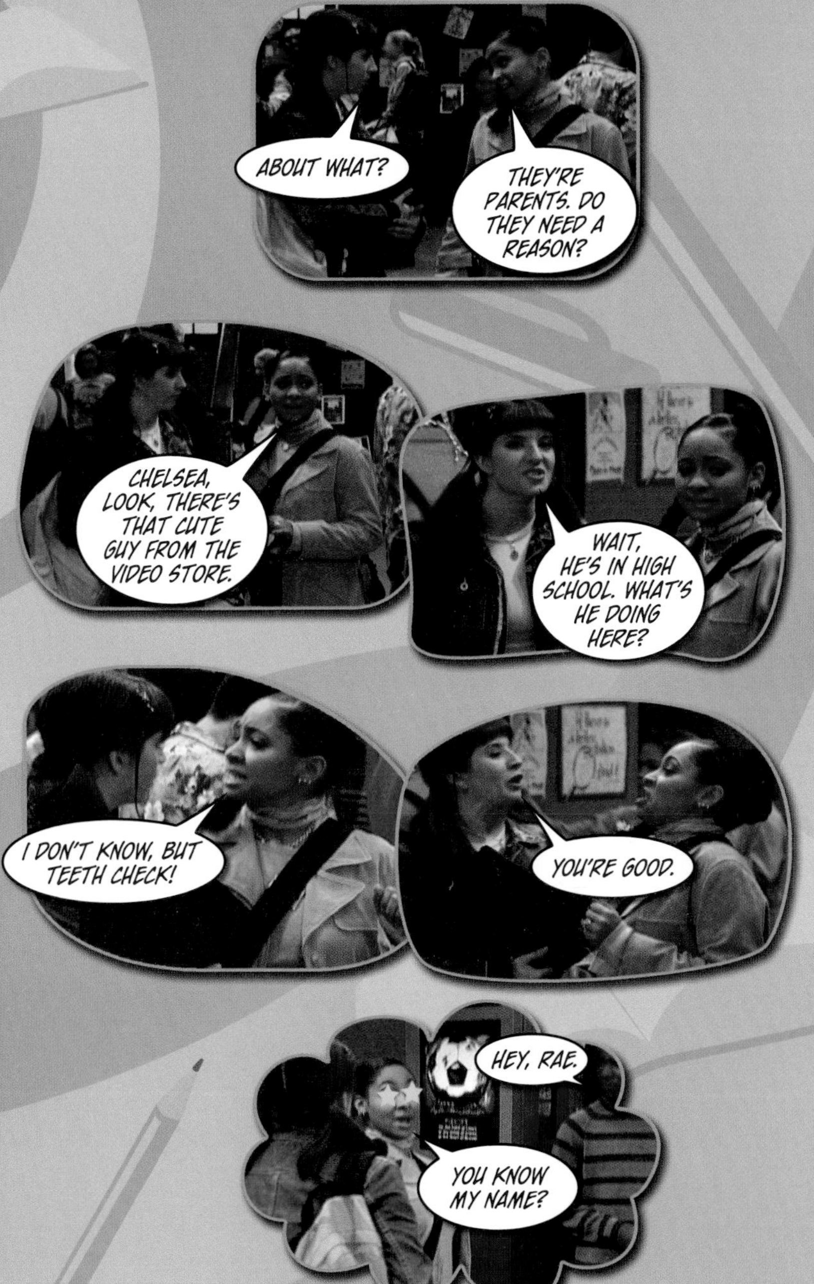
ABOUT WHAT?
THEY'RE PARENTS. DO THEY NEED A REASON?
CHELSEA, LOOK, THERE'S THAT CUTE GUY FROM THE VIDEO STORE.
WAIT, HE'S IN HIGH SCHOOL. WHAT'S HE DOING HERE?
I DON'T KNOW, BUT TEETH CHECK!
YOU'RE GOOD.
HEY, RAE.
YOU KNOW MY NAME?

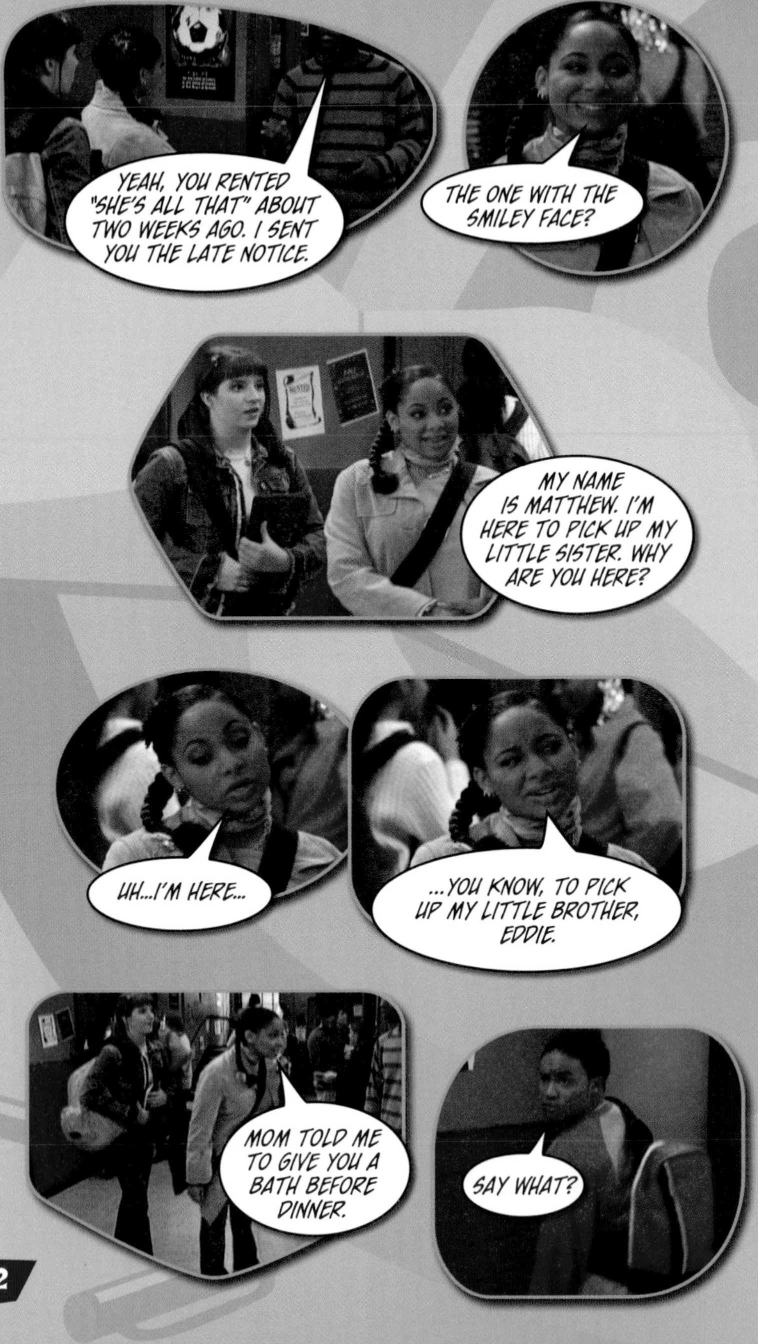
YEAH, YOU RENTED "SHE'S ALL THAT" ABOUT TWO WEEKS AGO. I SENT YOU THE LATE NOTICE.
THE ONE WITH THE SMILEY FACE?
MY NAME IS MATTHEW. I'M HERE TO PICK UP MY LITTLE SISTER. WHY ARE YOU HERE?
UH...I'M HERE...
...YOU KNOW, TO PICK UP MY LITTLE BROTHER, EDDIE.
MOM TOLD ME TO GIVE YOU A BATH BEFORE DINNER.
SAY WHAT?

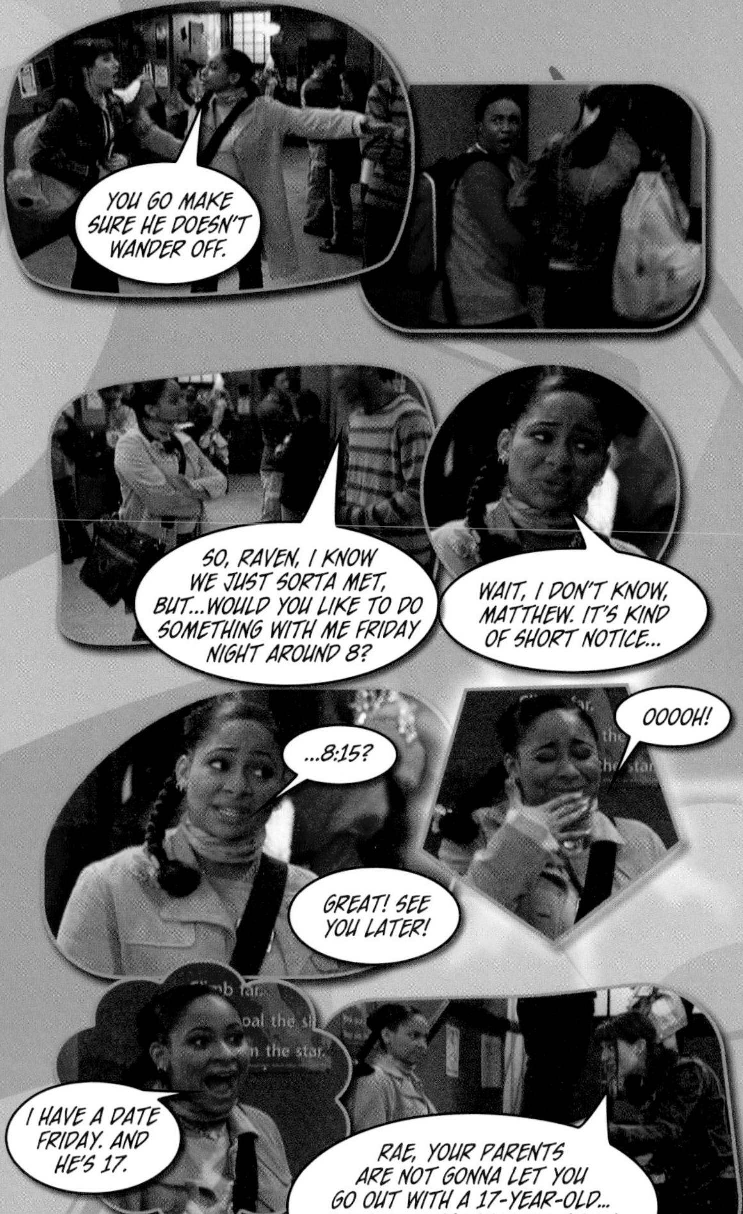
YOU GO MAKE SURE HE DOESN'T WANDER OFF.
SO, RAVEN, I KNOW WE JUST SORTA MET, BUT...WOULD YOU LIKE TO DO SOMETHING WITH ME FRIDAY NIGHT AROUND 8?
WAIT, I DON'T KNOW, MATTHEW. IT'S KIND OF SHORT NOTICE...
...8:15?
GREAT! SEE YOU LATER!
OOOOH!
I HAVE A DATE FRIDAY. AND HE'S 17.
RAE, YOUR PARENTS ARE NOT GONNA LET YOU GO OUT WITH A 17-YEAR-OLD... WAIT, RAE, THAT'S YOUR VISION. YOUR PARENTS ARE GONNA SAY, "NO."

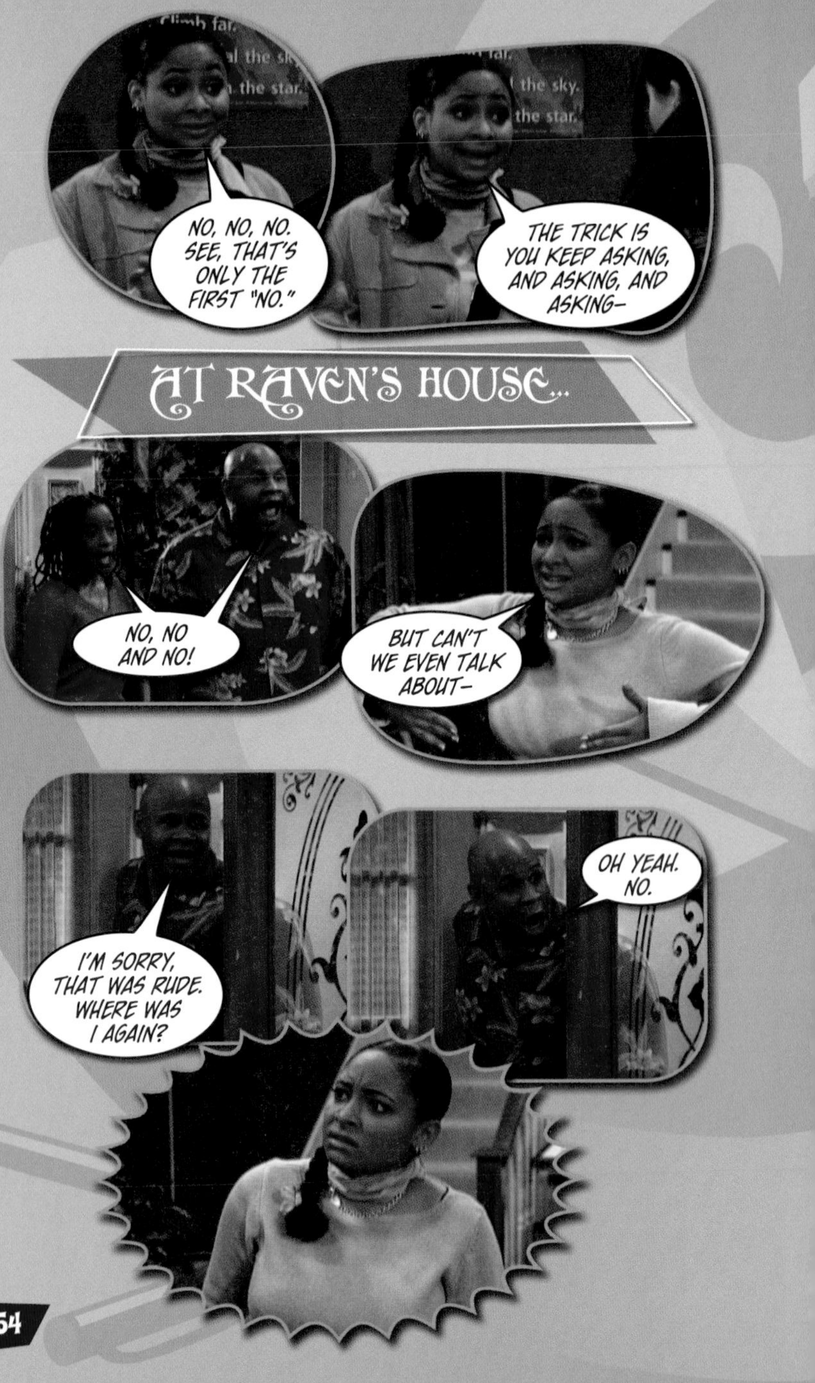
NO, NO, NO. SEE, THAT'S ONLY THE FIRST "NO."
THE TRICK IS YOU KEEP ASKING, AND ASKING, AND ASKING–
AT RAVEN'S HOUSE...
NO, NO AND NO!
BUT CAN'T WE EVEN TALK ABOUT–
I'M SORRY, THAT WAS RUDE. WHERE WAS I AGAIN?
OH YEAH. NO.

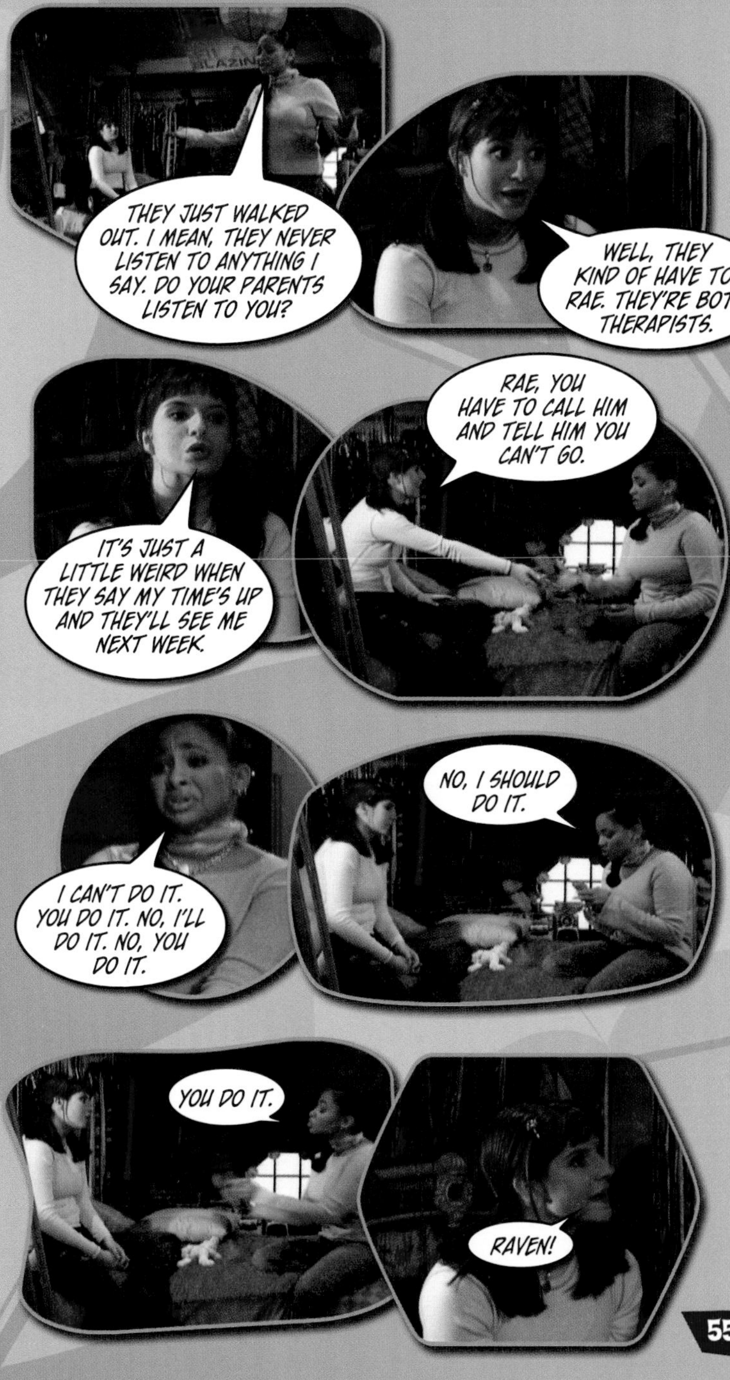
THEY JUST WALKED OUT. I MEAN, THEY NEVER LISTEN TO ANYTHING I SAY. DO YOUR PARENTS LISTEN TO YOU?
WELL, THEY KIND OF HAVE TO, RAE. THEY'RE BOTH THERAPISTS.
IT'S JUST A LITTLE WEIRD WHEN THEY SAY MY TIME'S UP AND THEY'LL SEE ME NEXT WEEK.
RAE, YOU HAVE TO CALL HIM AND TELL HIM YOU CAN'T GO.
I CAN'T DO IT. YOU DO IT. NO, I'LL DO IT. NO, YOU DO IT.
NO, I SHOULD DO IT.
YOU DO IT.
RAVEN!

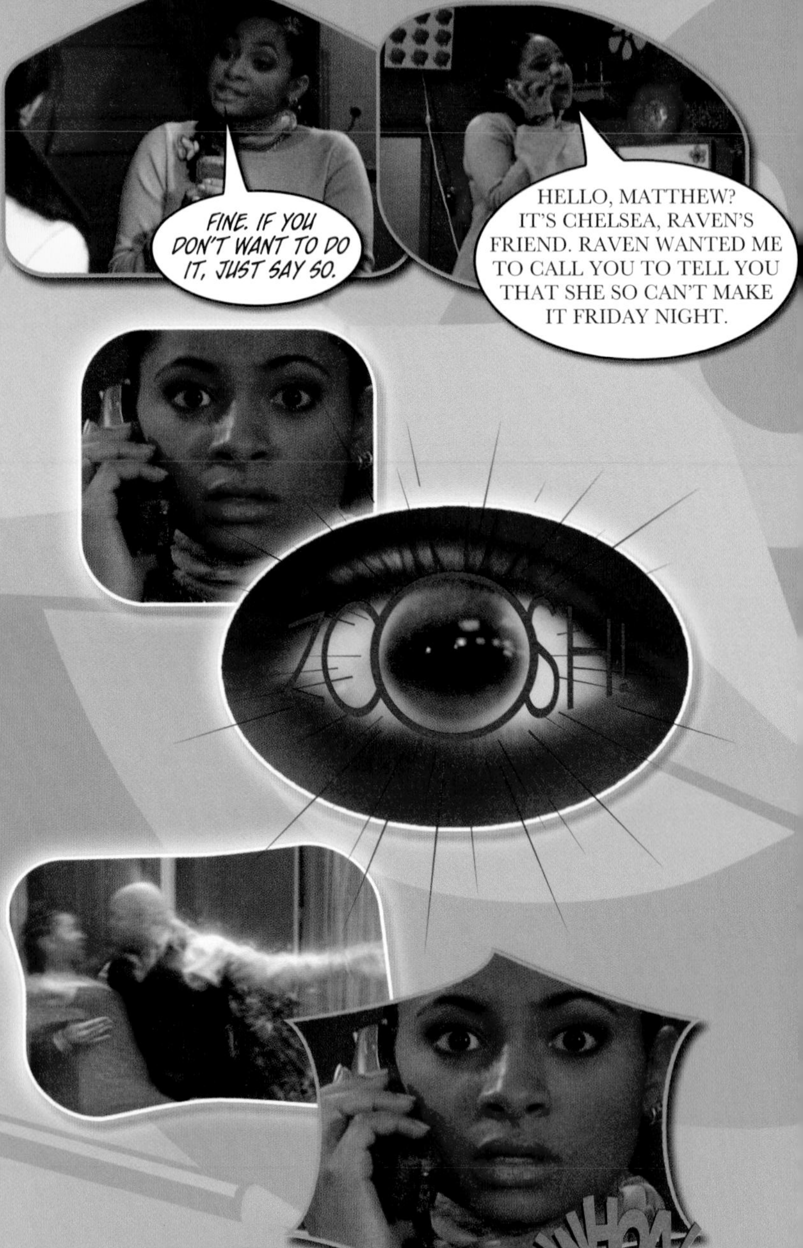

FINE. IF YOU DON'T WANT TO DO IT, JUST SAY SO.
HELLO, MATTHEW? IT'S CHELSEA, RAVEN'S FRIEND. RAVEN WANTED ME TO CALL YOU TO TELL YOU THAT SHE SO CAN'T MAKE IT FRIDAY NIGHT.
ZOOSH!
WHOA!

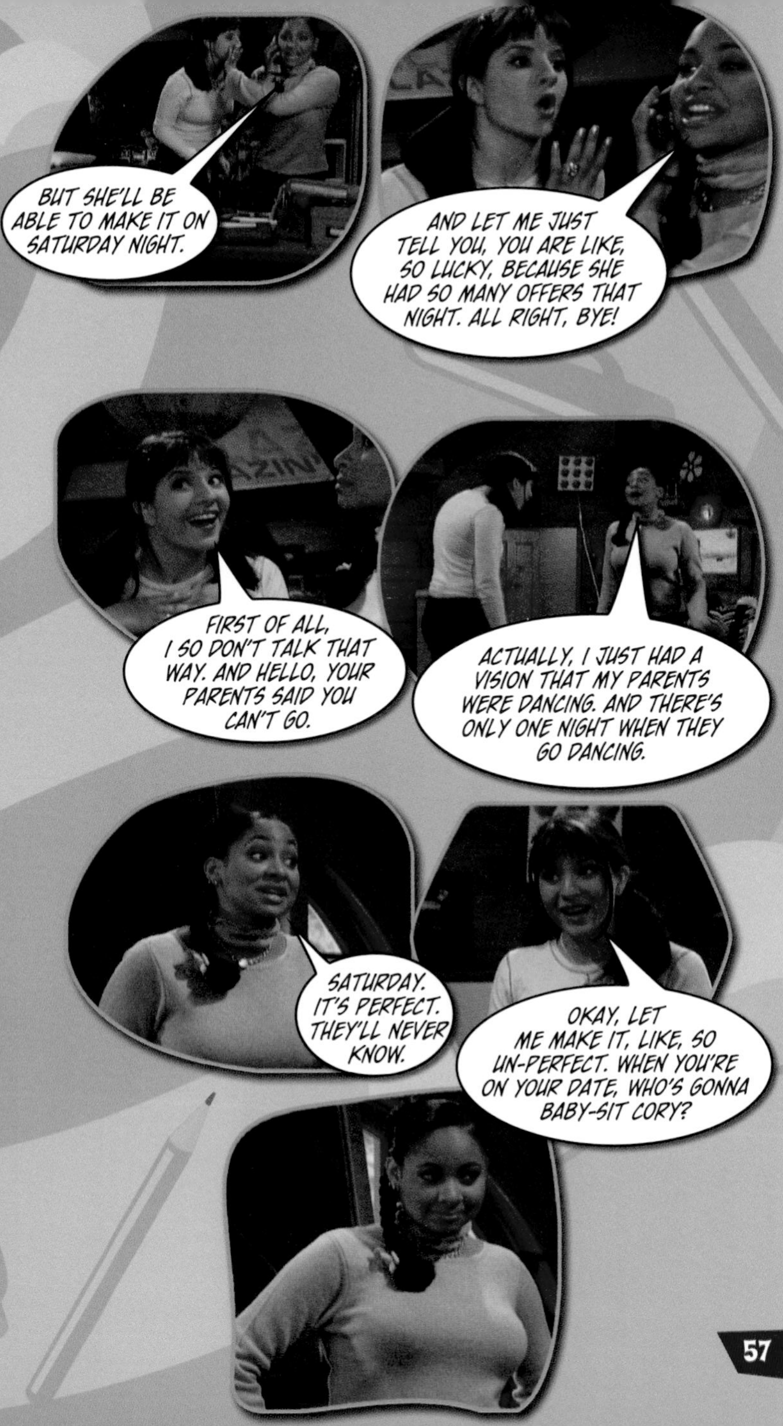
BUT SHE'LL BE ABLE TO MAKE IT ON SATURDAY NIGHT.
AND LET ME JUST TELL YOU, YOU ARE LIKE, SO LUCKY, BECAUSE SHE HAD SO MANY OFFERS THAT NIGHT. ALL RIGHT, BYE!
FIRST OF ALL, I SO DON'T TALK THAT WAY. AND HELLO, YOUR PARENTS SAID YOU CAN'T GO.
ACTUALLY, I JUST HAD A VISION THAT MY PARENTS WERE DANCING. AND THERE'S ONLY ONE NIGHT WHEN THEY GO DANCING.
SATURDAY. IT'S PERFECT. THEY'LL NEVER KNOW.
OKAY, LET ME MAKE IT, LIKE, SO UN-PERFECT. WHEN YOU'RE ON YOUR DATE, WHO'S GONNA BABY-SIT CORY?

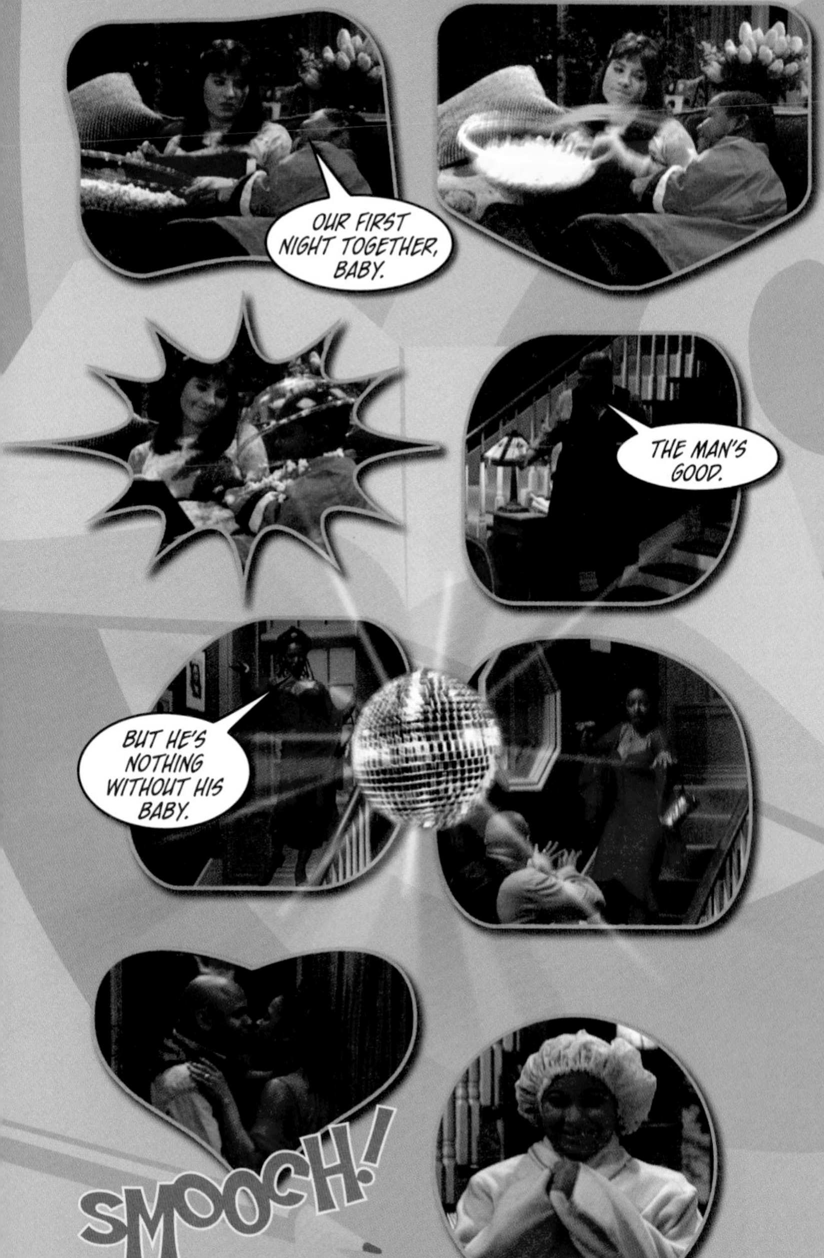

OUR FIRST NIGHT TOGETHER, BABY.
THE MAN'S GOOD.
BUT HE'S NOTHING WITHOUT HIS BABY.
SMOOCH!

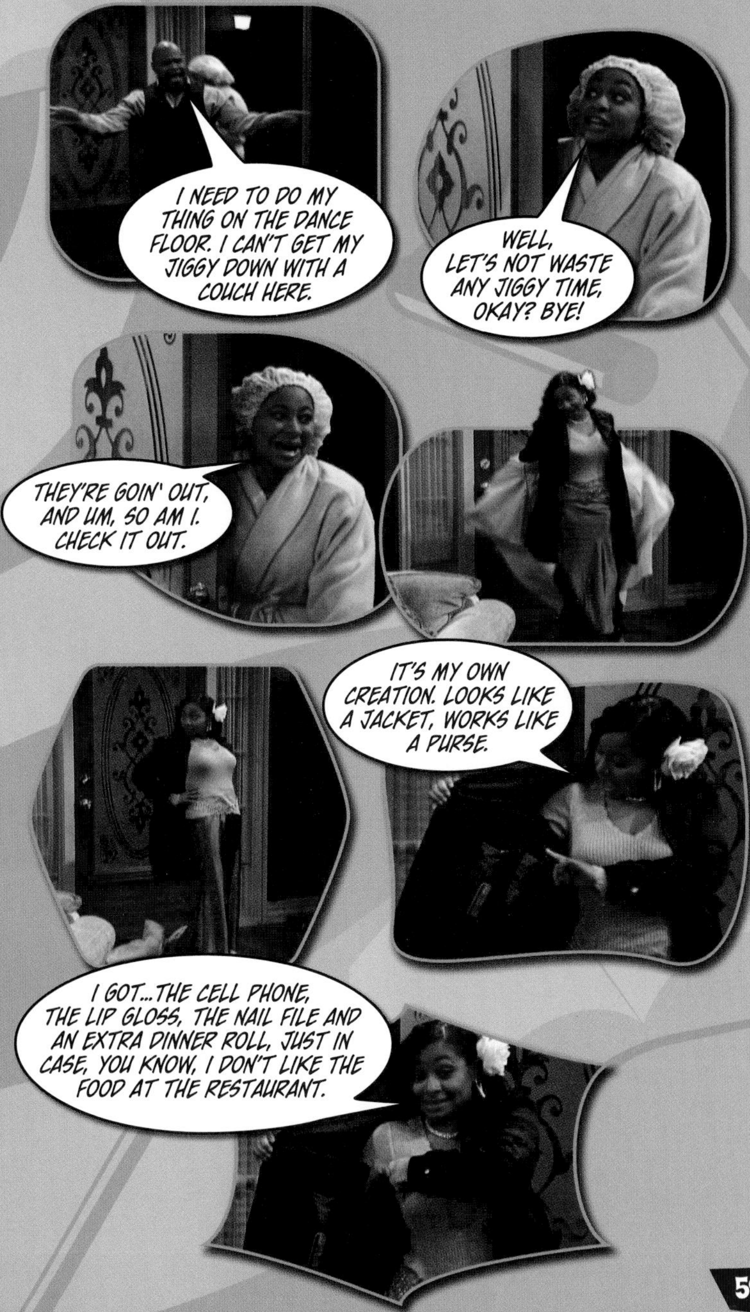
I NEED TO DO MY THING ON THE DANCE FLOOR. I CAN'T GET MY JIGGY DOWN WITH A COUCH HERE.
WELL, LET'S NOT WASTE ANY JIGGY TIME, OKAY? BYE!
THEY'RE GOIN' OUT, AND UM, SO AM I. CHECK IT OUT.
IT'S MY OWN CREATION. LOOKS LIKE A JACKET, WORKS LIKE A PURSE.
I GOT...THE CELL PHONE, THE LIP GLOSS, THE NAIL FILE AND AN EXTRA DINNER ROLL, JUST IN CASE, YOU KNOW, I DON'T LIKE THE FOOD AT THE RESTAURANT.

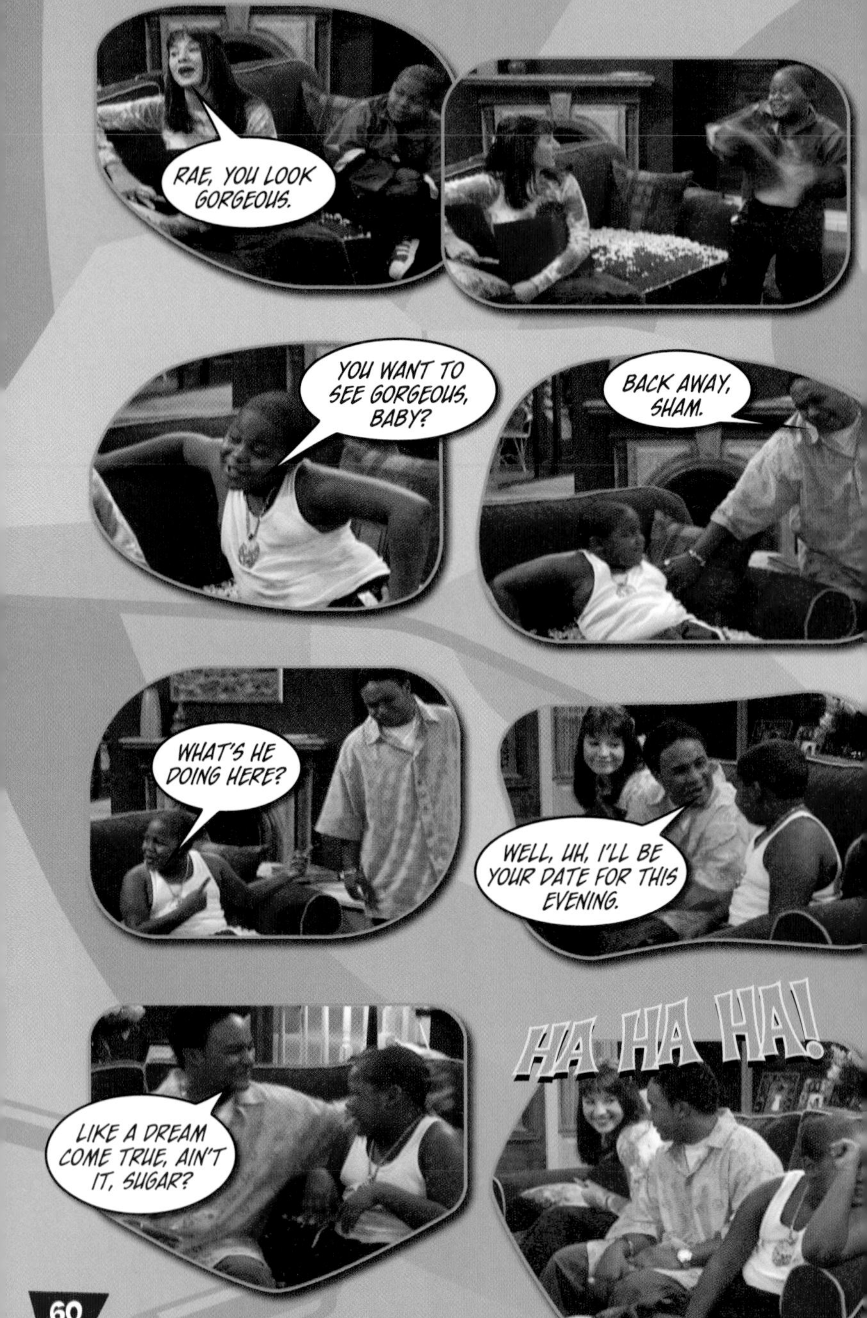
RAE, YOU LOOK GORGEOUS.
YOU WANT TO SEE GORGEOUS, BABY?
BACK AWAY, SHAM.
WHAT'S HE DOING HERE?
WELL, UH, I'LL BE YOUR DATE FOR THIS EVENING.
LIKE A DREAM COME TRUE, AIN'T IT, SUGAR?
HA HA HA!

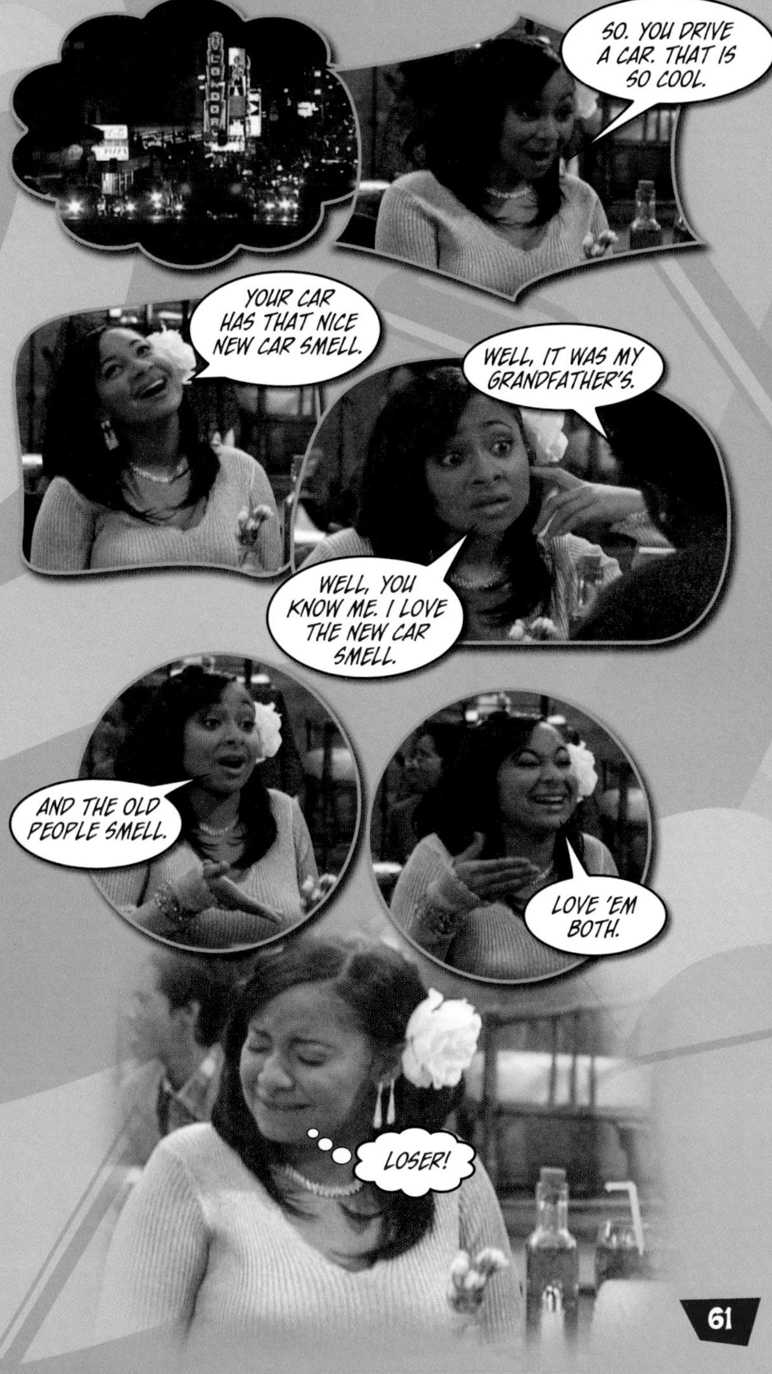
SO. YOU DRIVE A CAR. THAT IS SO COOL.
YOUR CAR HAS THAT NICE NEW CAR SMELL.
WELL, IT WAS MY GRANDFATHER'S.
WELL, YOU KNOW ME. I LOVE THE NEW CAR SMELL.
AND THE OLD PEOPLE SMELL.
LOVE 'EM BOTH.
LOSER!

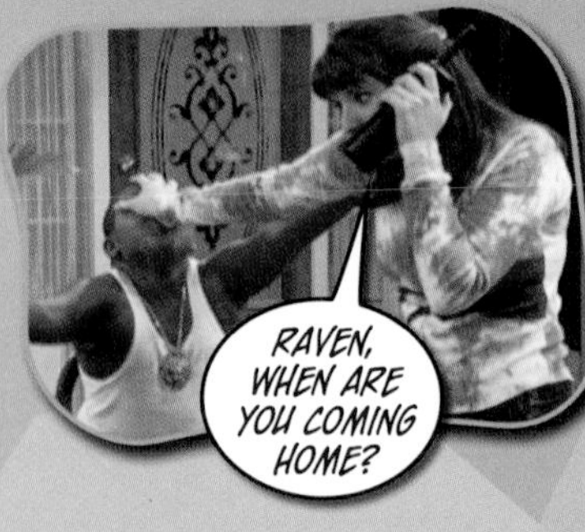
RAVEN, WHEN ARE YOU COMING HOME?

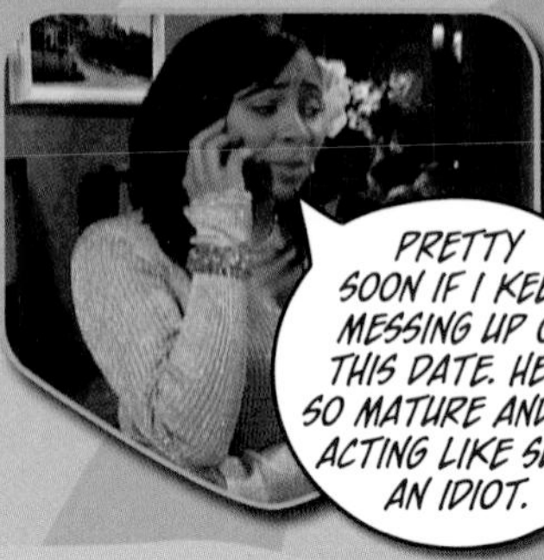
PRETTY SOON IF I KEEP MESSING UP ON THIS DATE. HE IS SO MATURE AND I'M ACTING LIKE SUCH AN IDIOT.

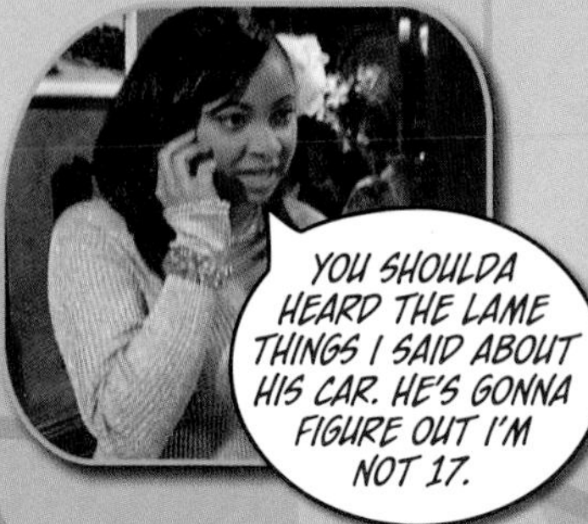
YOU SHOULDA HEARD THE LAME THINGS I SAID ABOUT HIS CAR. HE'S GONNA FIGURE OUT I'M NOT 17.

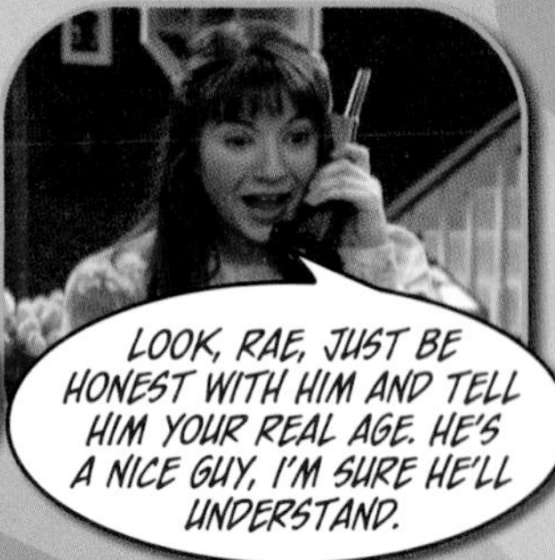
LOOK, RAE, JUST BE HONEST WITH HIM AND TELL HIM YOUR REAL AGE. HE'S A NICE GUY, I'M SURE HE'LL UNDERSTAND.

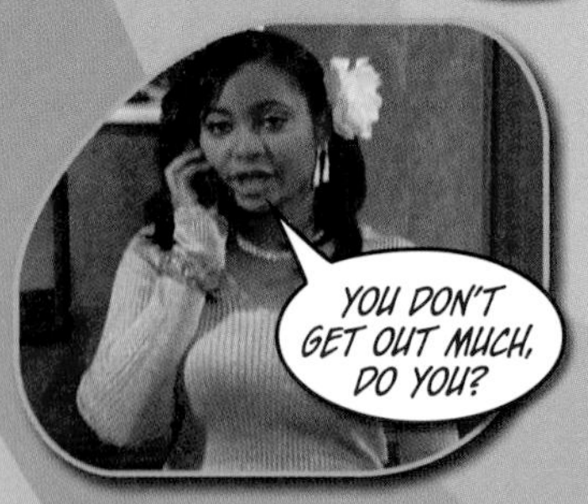
YOU DON'T GET OUT MUCH, DO YOU?

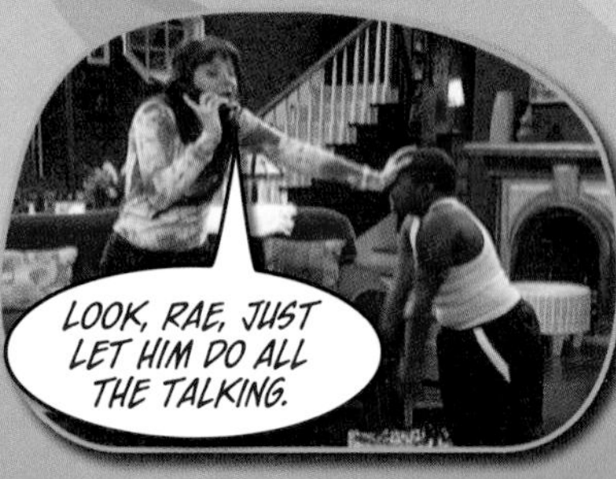
LOOK, RAE, JUST LET HIM DO ALL THE TALKING.

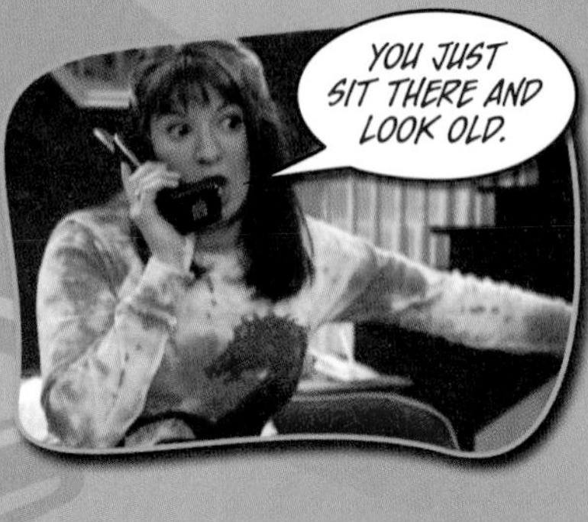
YOU JUST SIT THERE AND LOOK OLD.

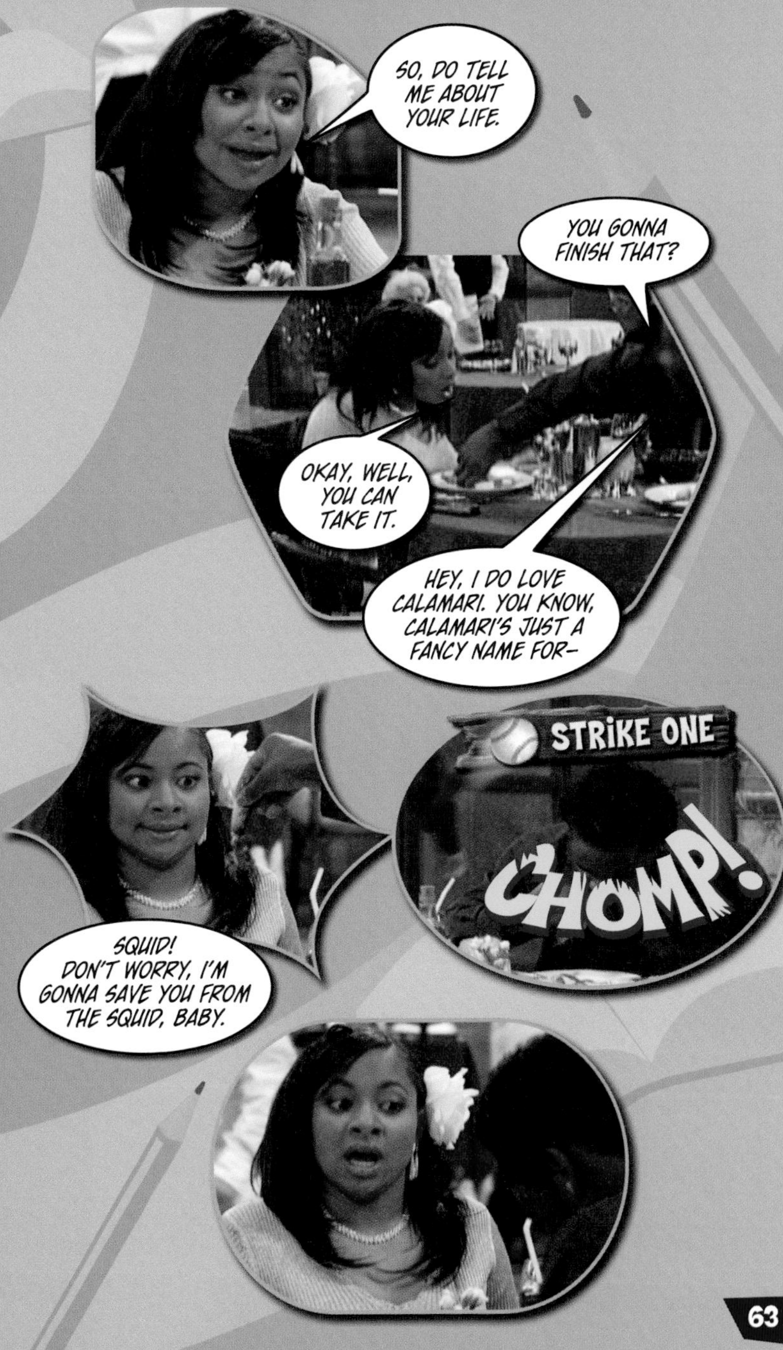
SO, DO TELL ME ABOUT YOUR LIFE.
YOU GONNA FINISH THAT?
OKAY, WELL, YOU CAN TAKE IT.
HEY, I DO LOVE CALAMARI. YOU KNOW, CALAMARI'S JUST A FANCY NAME FOR–
SQUID! DON'T WORRY, I'M GONNA SAVE YOU FROM THE SQUID, BABY.
STRIKE ONE
CHOMP!

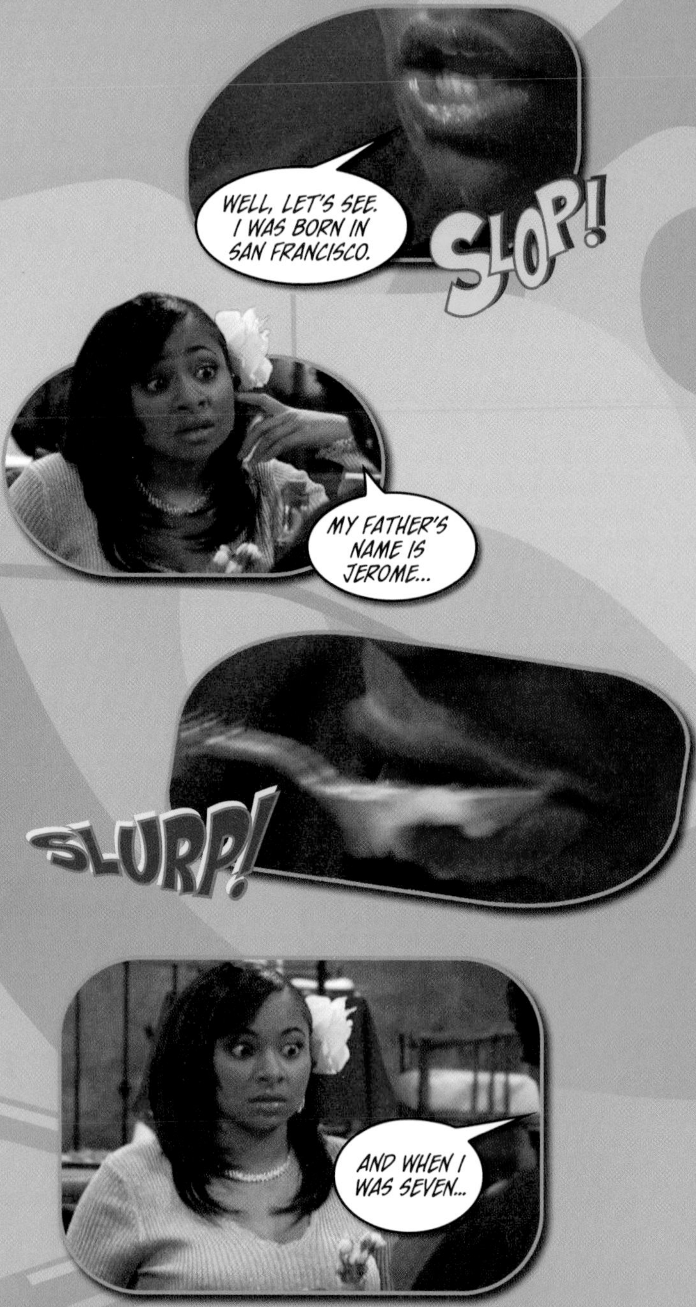
WELL, LET'S SEE. I WAS BORN IN SAN FRANCISCO.
SLOP!
MY FATHER'S NAME IS JEROME...
SLURP!
AND WHEN I WAS SEVEN...

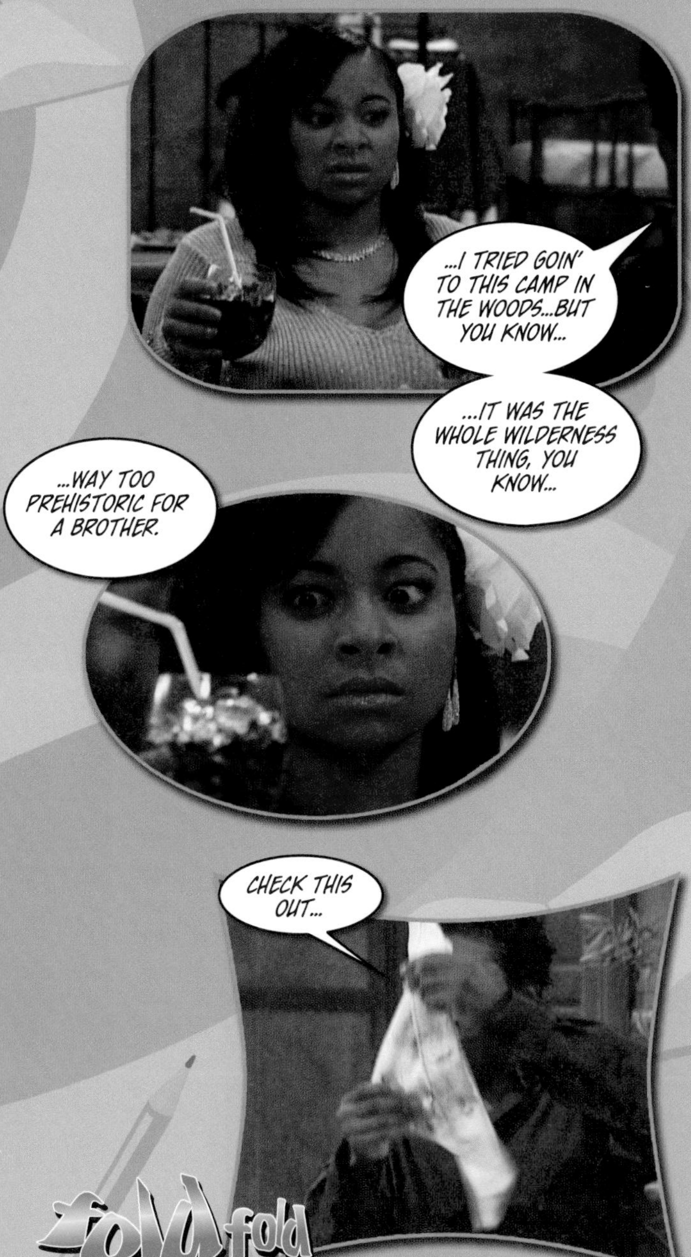
...I TRIED GOIN' TO THIS CAMP IN THE WOODS...BUT YOU KNOW...
...IT WAS THE WHOLE WILDERNESS THING, YOU KNOW...
...WAY TOO PREHISTORIC FOR A BROTHER.
CHECK THIS OUT...

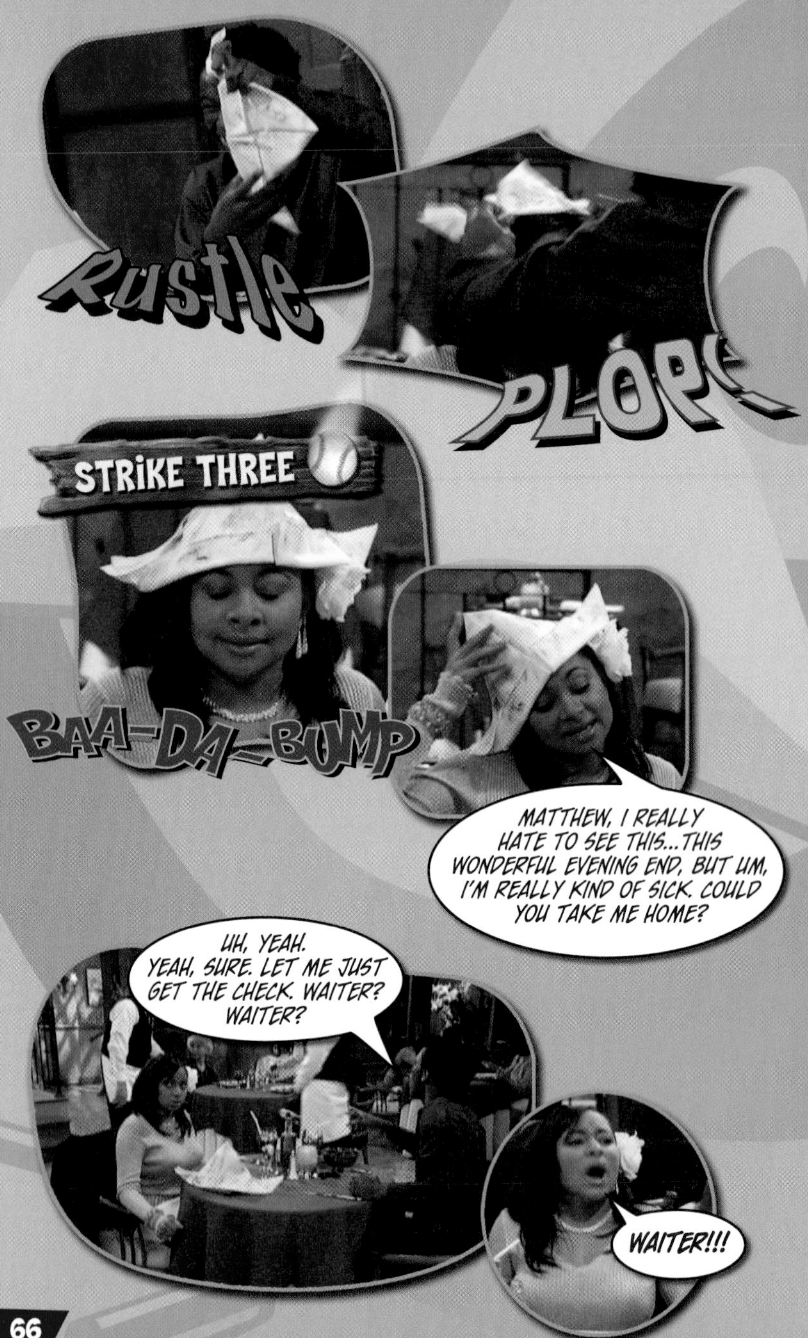
Rustle
PLOP!
STRIKE THREE
BAA-DA-BUMP
MATTHEW, I REALLY HATE TO SEE THIS...THIS WONDERFUL EVENING END, BUT UM, I'M REALLY KIND OF SICK. COULD YOU TAKE ME HOME?
UH, YEAH. YEAH, SURE. LET ME JUST GET THE CHECK. WAITER? WAITER?
WAITER!!!

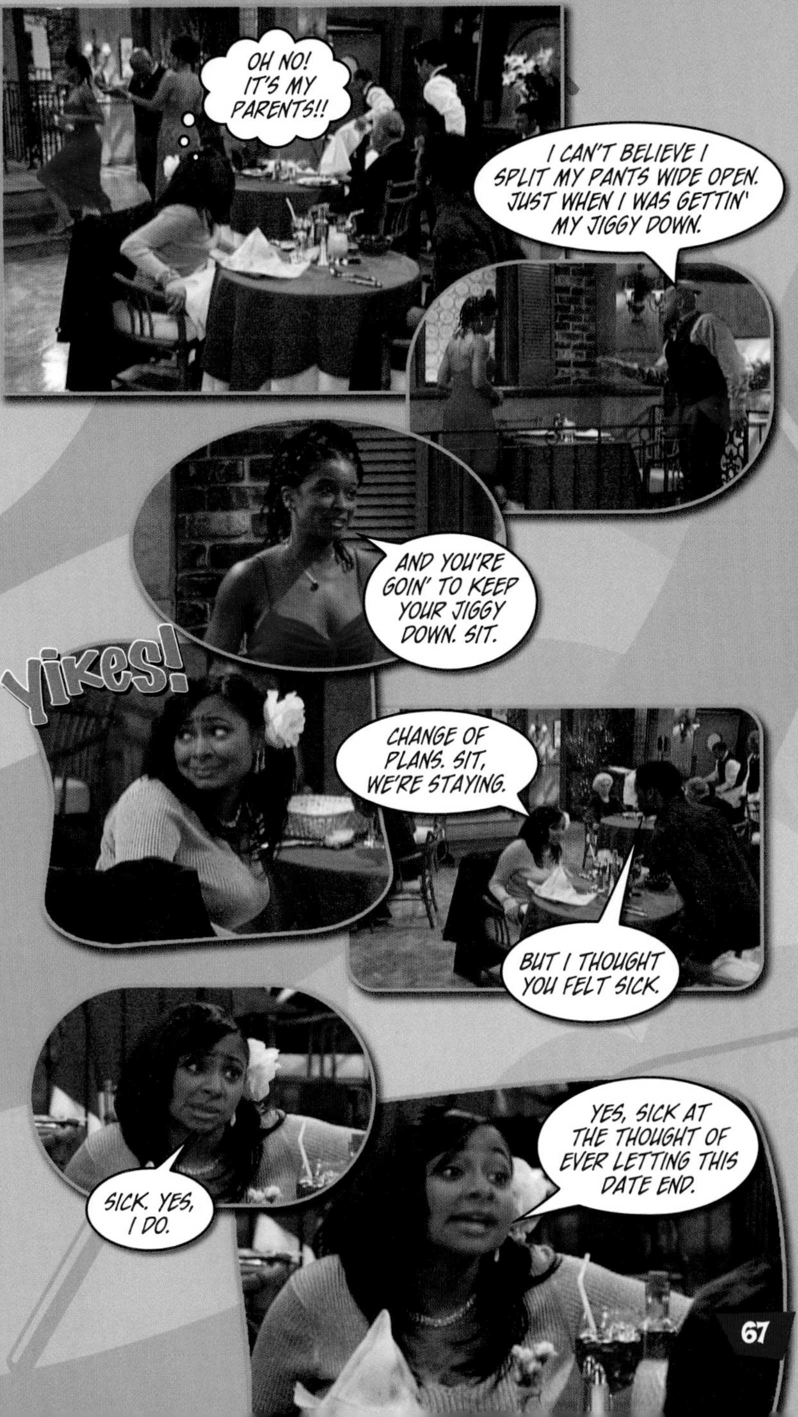
OH NO! IT'S MY PARENTS!!
I CAN'T BELIEVE I SPLIT MY PANTS WIDE OPEN. JUST WHEN I WAS GETTIN' MY JIGGY DOWN.
AND YOU'RE GOIN' TO KEEP YOUR JIGGY DOWN. SIT.
YIKES!
CHANGE OF PLANS. SIT, WE'RE STAYING.
BUT I THOUGHT YOU FELT SICK.
SICK. YES, I DO.
YES, SICK AT THE THOUGHT OF EVER LETTING THIS DATE END.

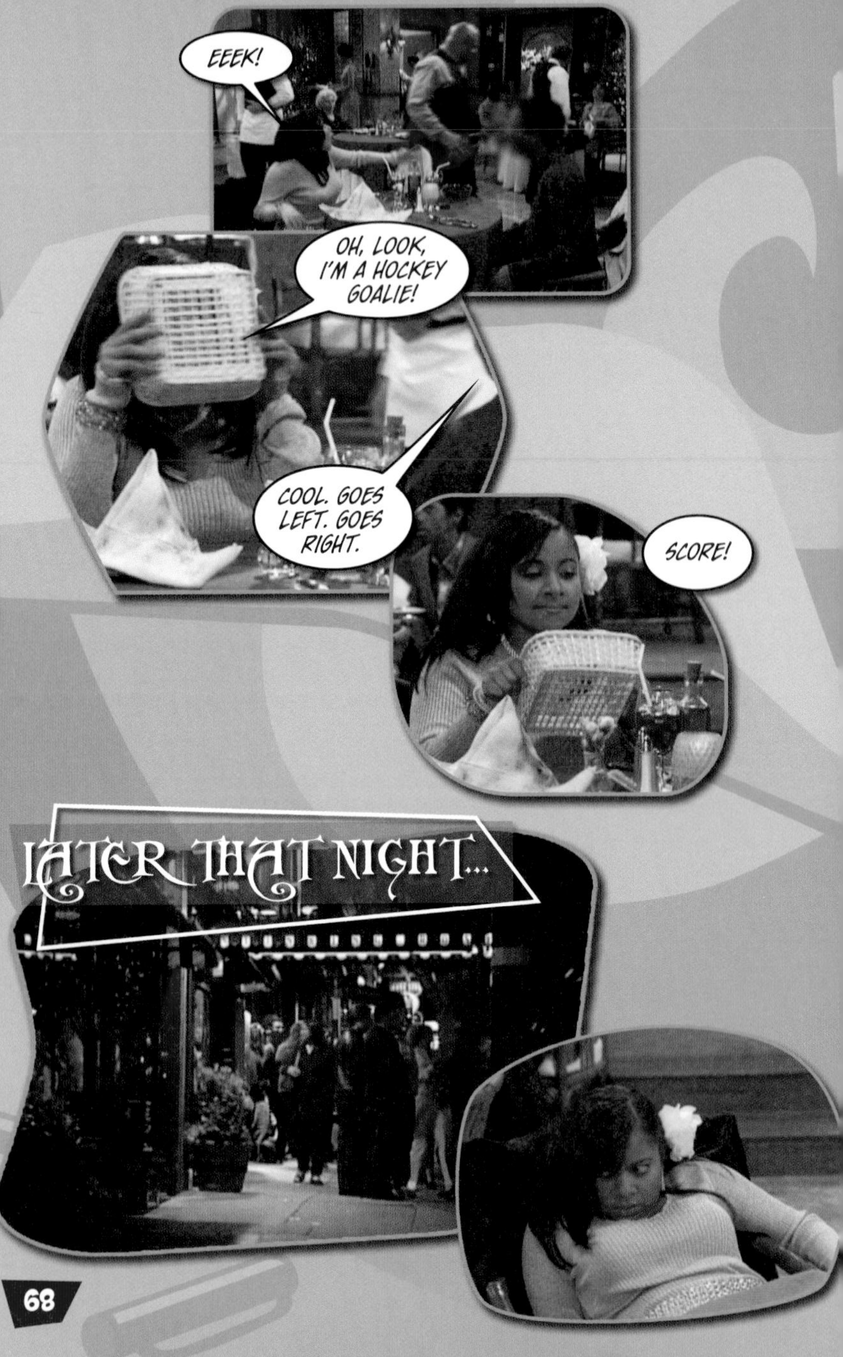
EEEK!
OH, LOOK, I'M A HOCKEY GOALIE!
COOL. GOES LEFT. GOES RIGHT.
SCORE!
LATER THAT NIGHT...

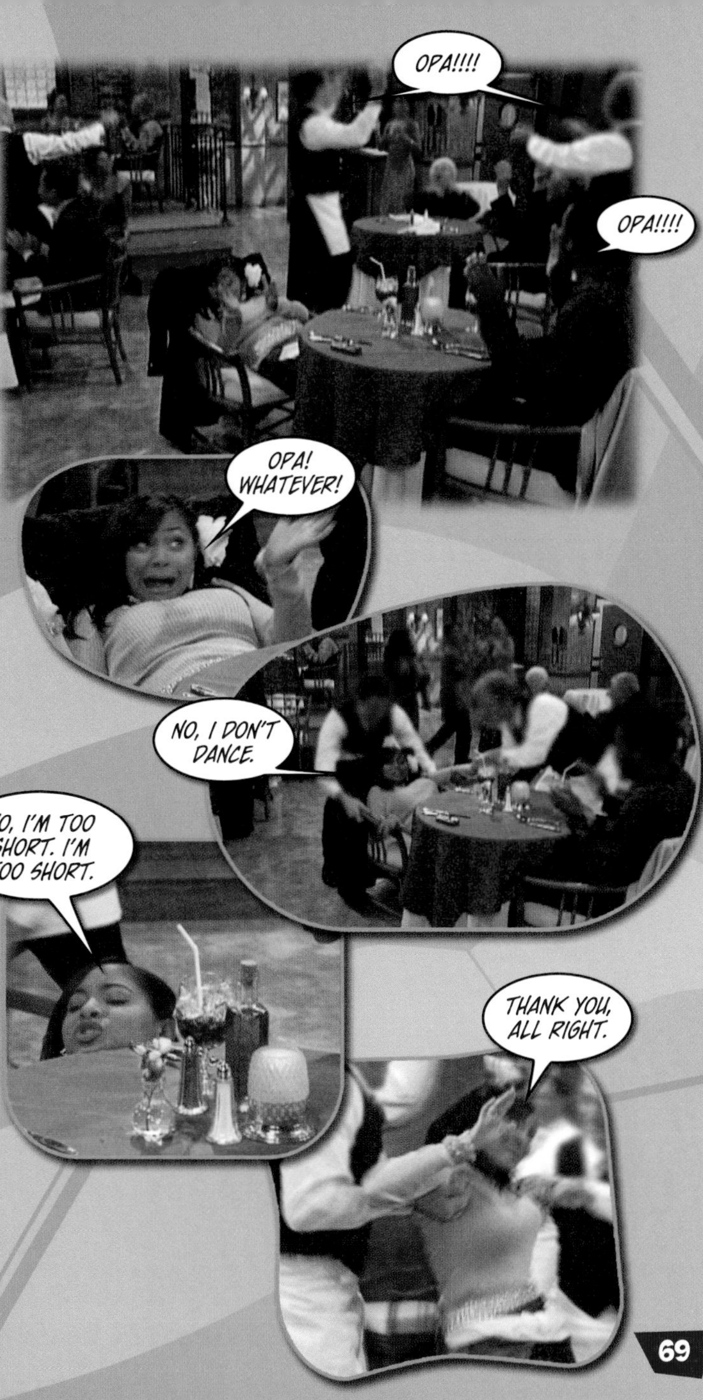
OPA!!!!
OPA!!!!
OPA! WHATEVER!
NO, I DON'T DANCE.
NO, I'M TOO SHORT. I'M TOO SHORT.
THANK YOU, ALL RIGHT.

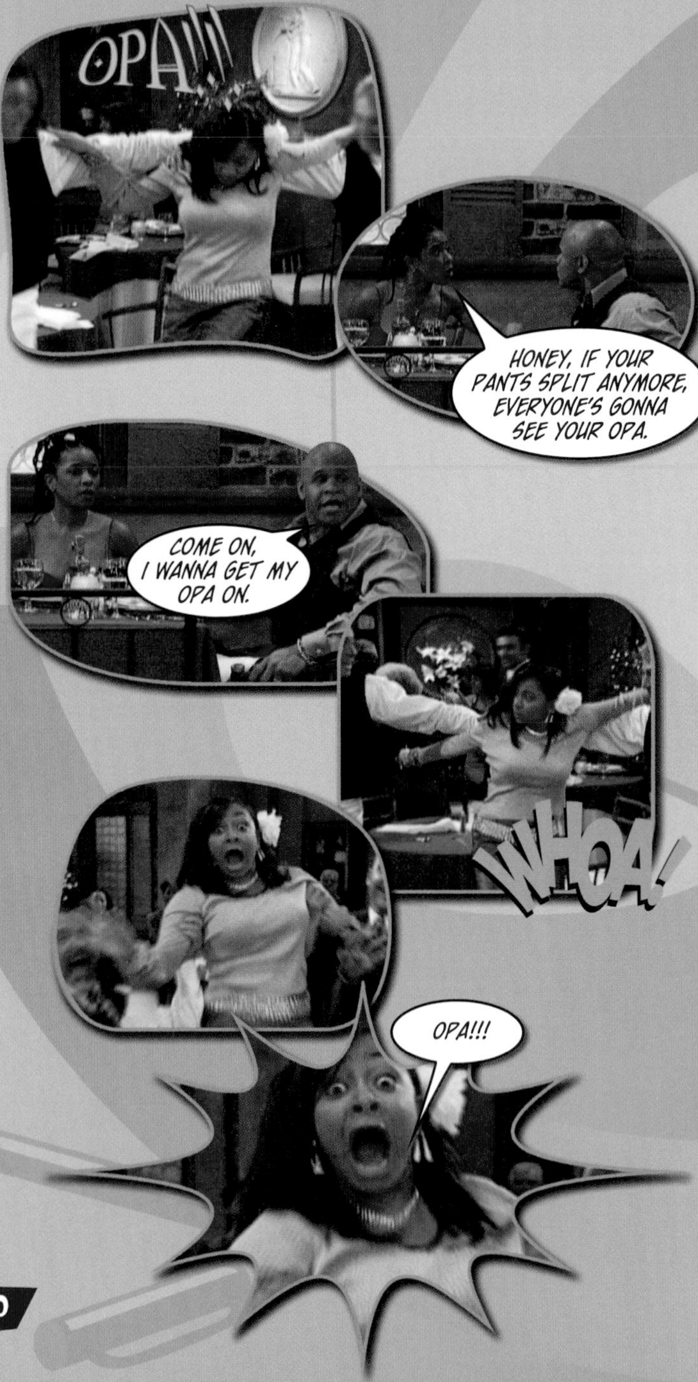
OPA!!!
HONEY, IF YOUR PANTS SPLIT ANYMORE, EVERYONE'S GONNA SEE YOUR OPA.
COME ON, I WANNA GET MY OPA ON.
WHOA!
OPA!!!

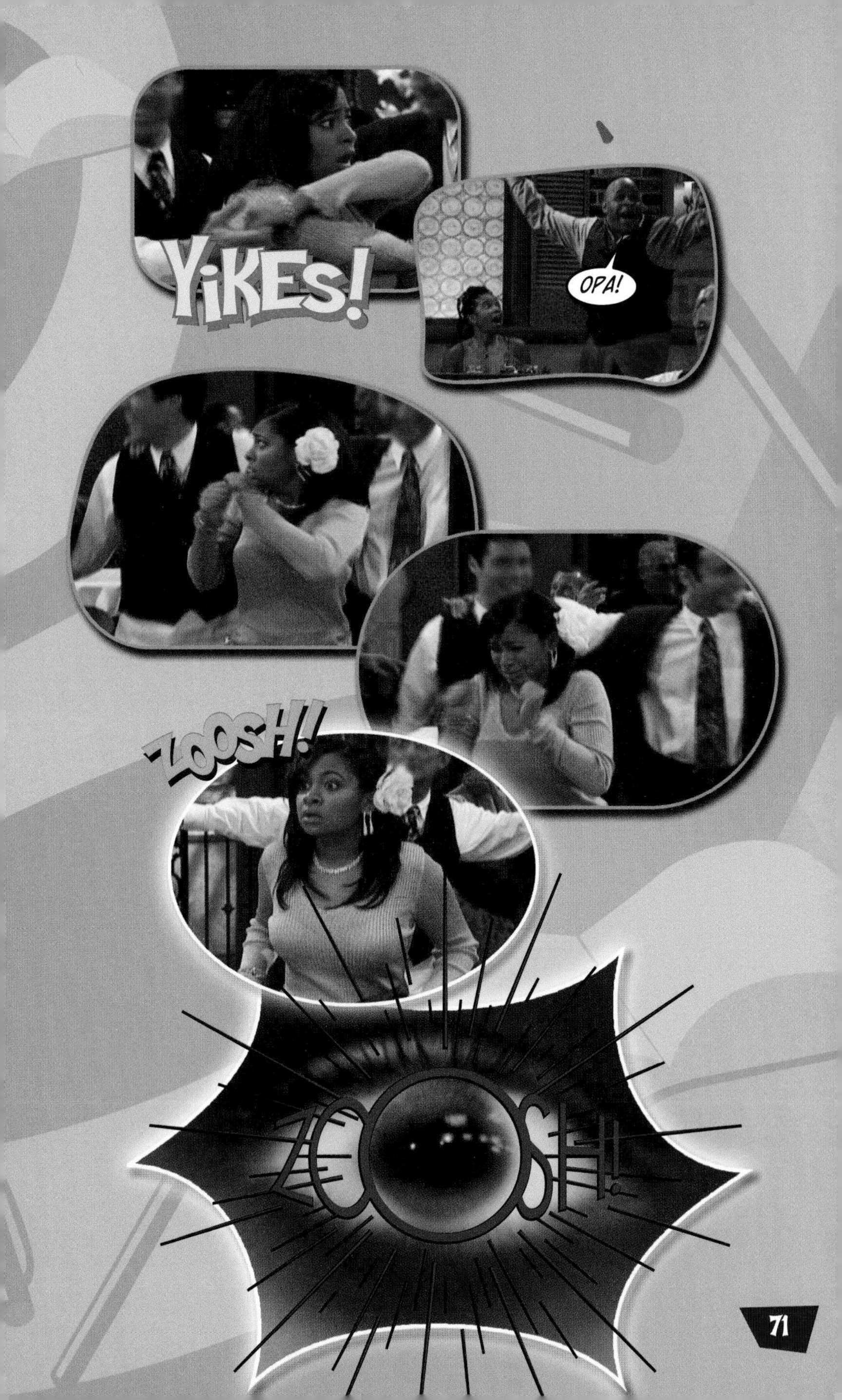
YIKES!
OPA!
ZOOSH!
ZOOSH!

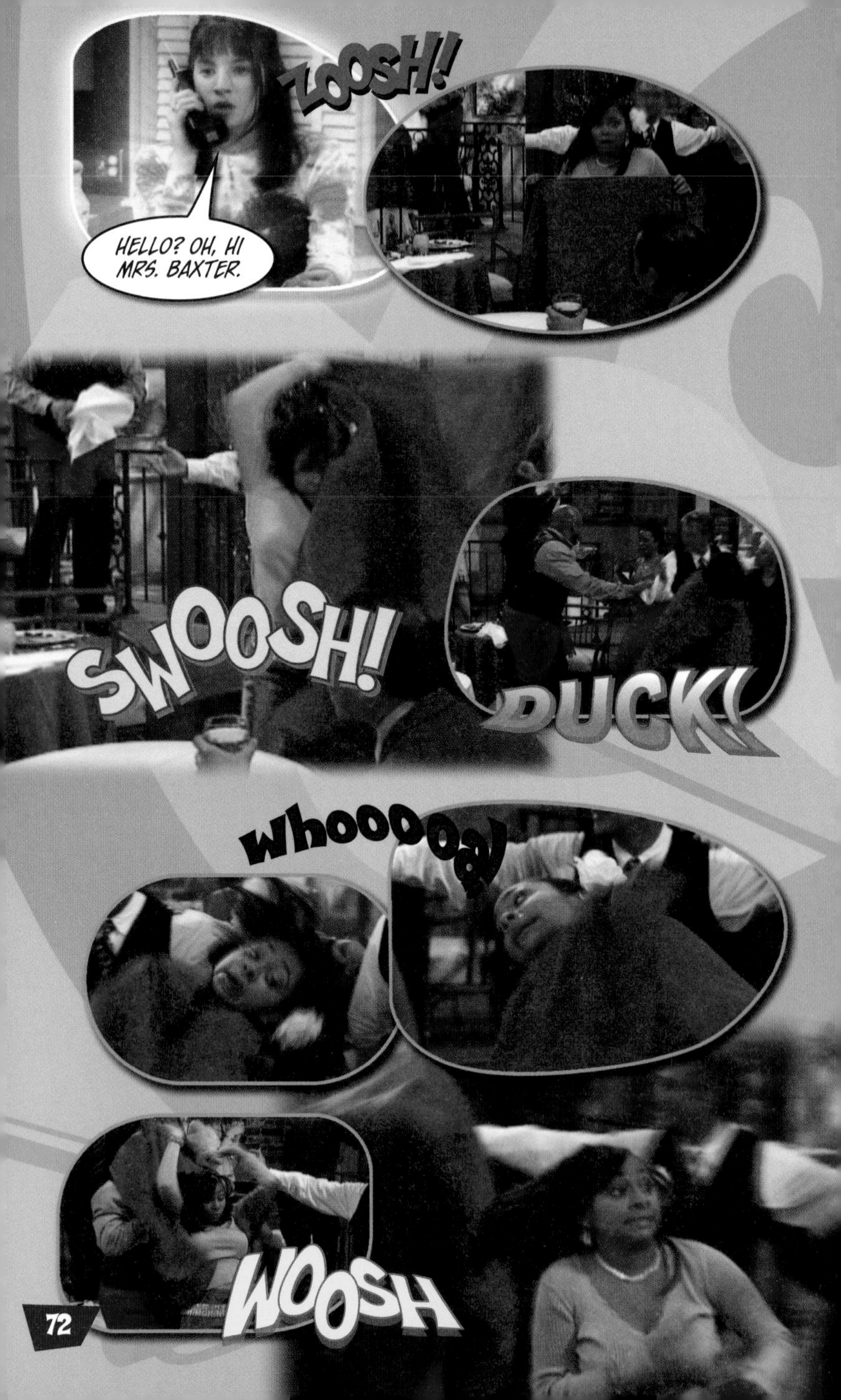
HELLO? OH, HI MRS. BAXTER.
ZOOSH!
SWOOSH!
DUCK!
Whooooa!
WOOSH

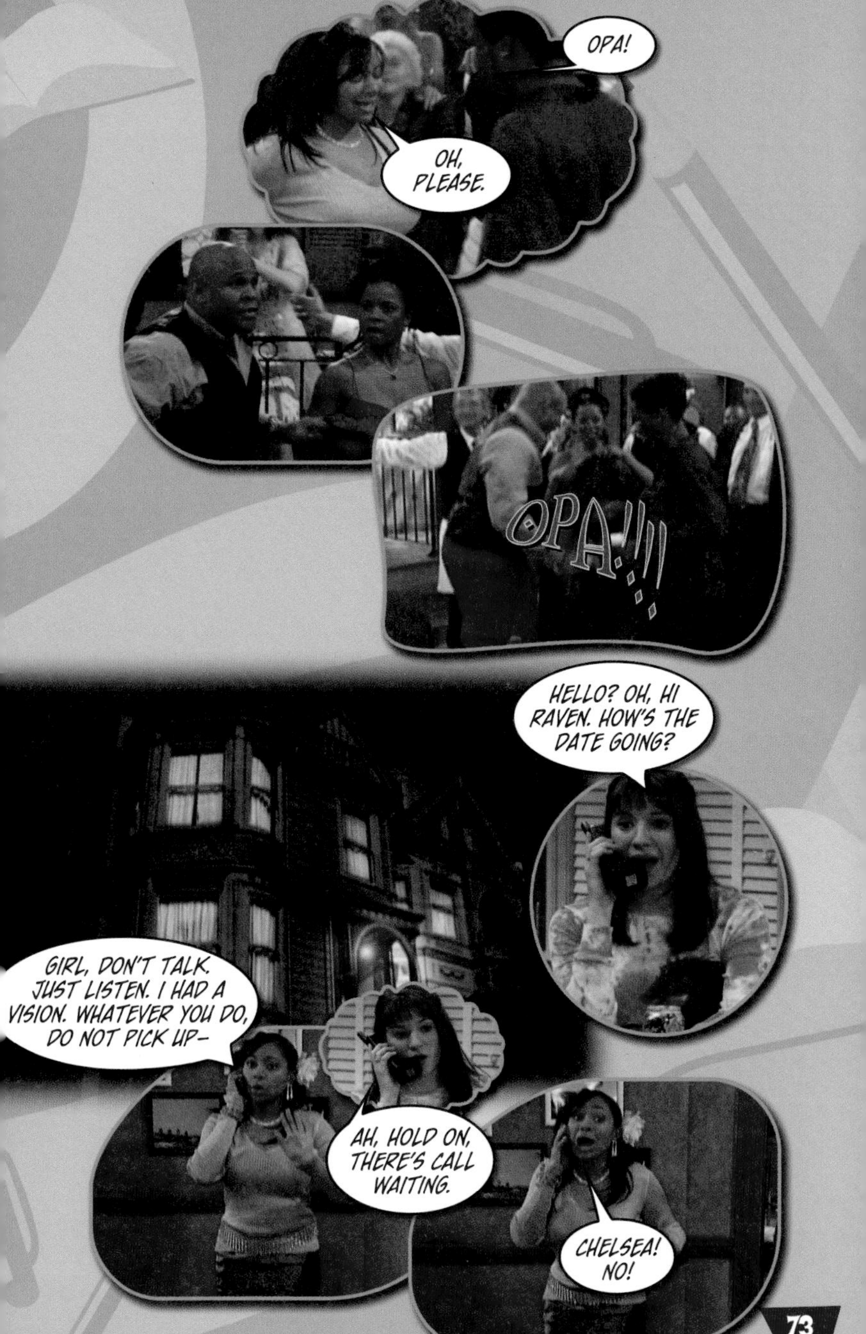
OPA!
OH, PLEASE.
OPA!!!!
HELLO? OH, HI RAVEN. HOW'S THE DATE GOING?
GIRL, DON'T TALK. JUST LISTEN. I HAD A VISION. WHATEVER YOU DO, DO NOT PICK UP–
AH, HOLD ON, THERE'S CALL WAITING.
CHELSEA! NO!

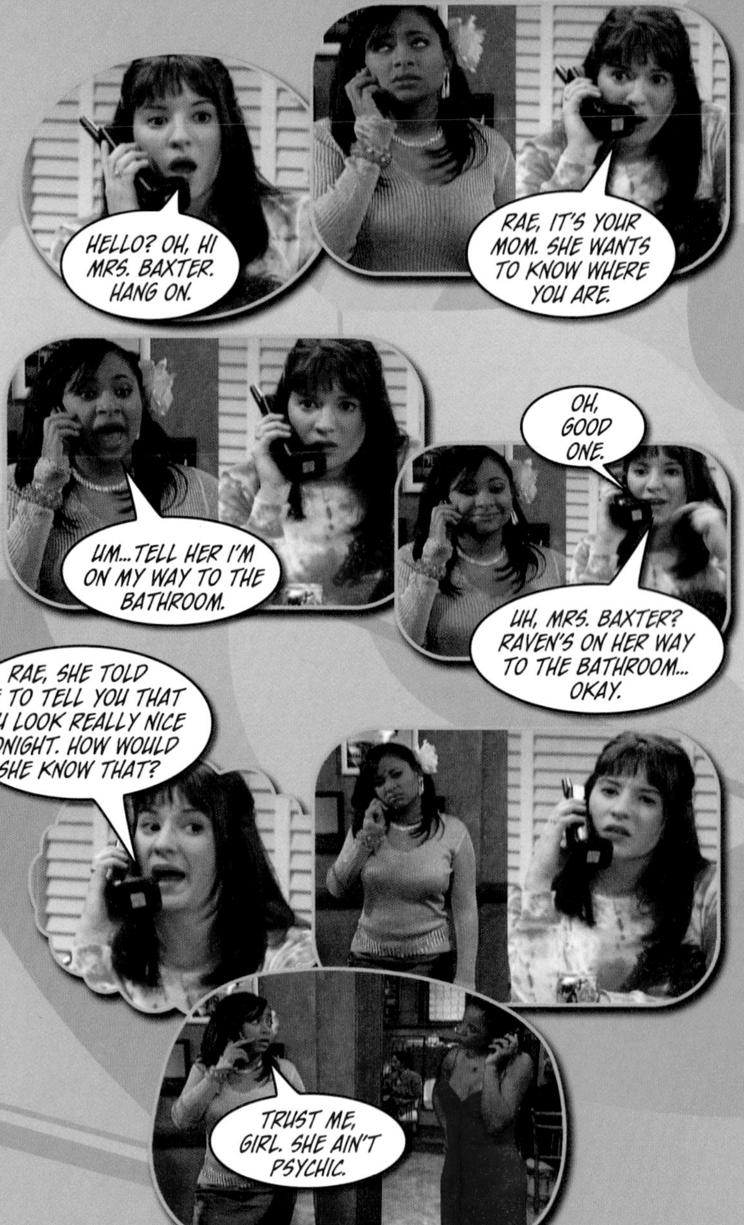
HELLO? OH, HI MRS. BAXTER. HANG ON.
RAE, IT'S YOUR MOM. SHE WANTS TO KNOW WHERE YOU ARE.
UM...TELL HER I'M ON MY WAY TO THE BATHROOM.
OH, GOOD ONE.
UH, MRS. BAXTER? RAVEN'S ON HER WAY TO THE BATHROOM... OKAY.
RAE, SHE TOLD ME TO TELL YOU THAT YOU LOOK REALLY NICE TONIGHT. HOW WOULD SHE KNOW THAT?
TRUST ME, GIRL. SHE AIN'T PSYCHIC.

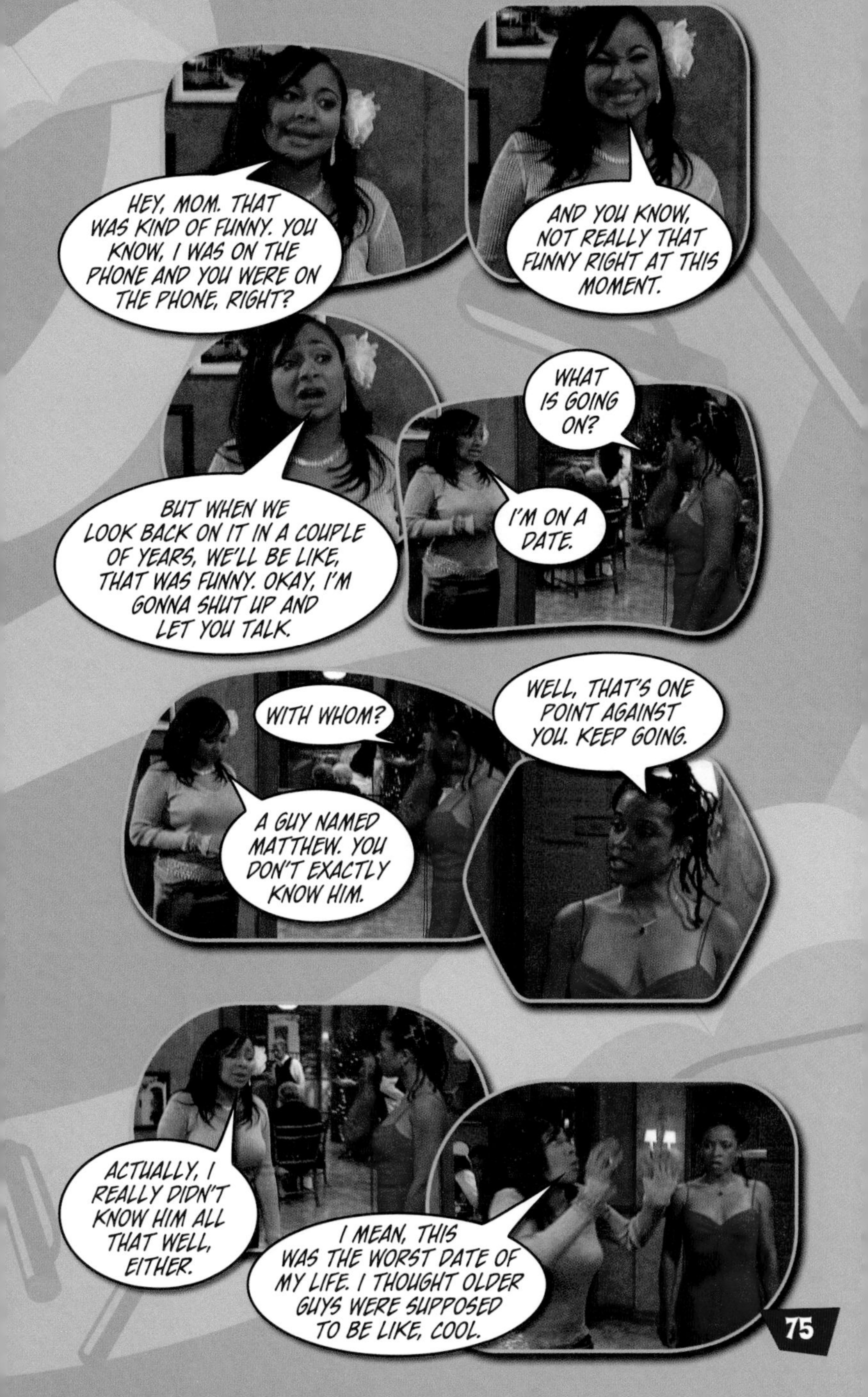
HEY, MOM. THAT WAS KIND OF FUNNY. YOU KNOW, I WAS ON THE PHONE AND YOU WERE ON THE PHONE, RIGHT?
AND YOU KNOW, NOT REALLY THAT FUNNY RIGHT AT THIS MOMENT.
BUT WHEN WE LOOK BACK ON IT IN A COUPLE OF YEARS, WE'LL BE LIKE, THAT WAS FUNNY. OKAY, I'M GONNA SHUT UP AND LET YOU TALK.
WHAT IS GOING ON?
I'M ON A DATE.
WITH WHOM?
A GUY NAMED MATTHEW. YOU DON'T EXACTLY KNOW HIM.
WELL, THAT'S ONE POINT AGAINST YOU. KEEP GOING.
ACTUALLY, I REALLY DIDN'T KNOW HIM ALL THAT WELL, EITHER.
I MEAN, THIS WAS THE WORST DATE OF MY LIFE. I THOUGHT OLDER GUYS WERE SUPPOSED TO BE LIKE, COOL.

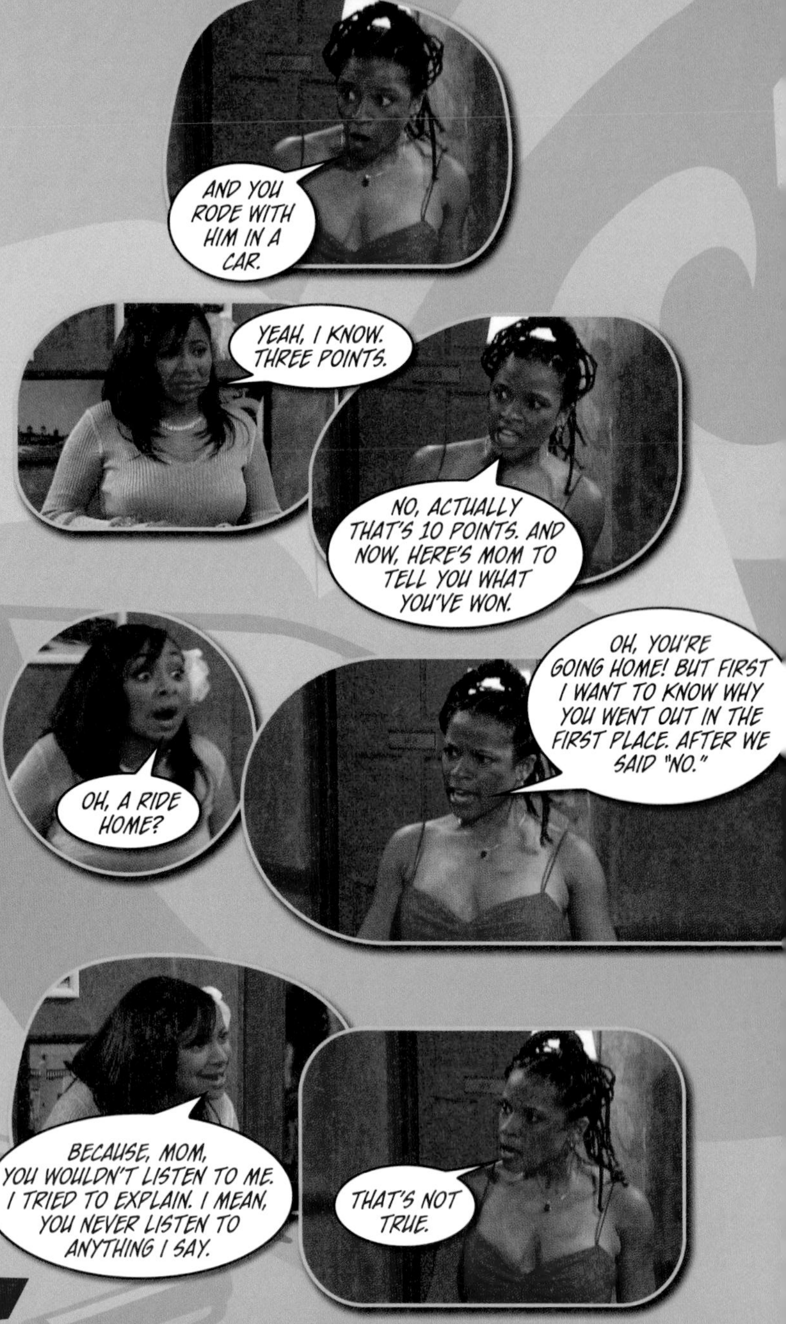

AND YOU RODE WITH HIM IN A CAR.
YEAH, I KNOW. THREE POINTS.
NO, ACTUALLY THAT'S 10 POINTS. AND NOW, HERE'S MOM TO TELL YOU WHAT YOU'VE WON.
OH, A RIDE HOME?
OH, YOU'RE GOING HOME! BUT FIRST I WANT TO KNOW WHY YOU WENT OUT IN THE FIRST PLACE. AFTER WE SAID "NO."
BECAUSE, MOM, YOU WOULDN'T LISTEN TO ME. I TRIED TO EXPLAIN. I MEAN, YOU NEVER LISTEN TO ANYTHING I SAY.
THAT'S NOT TRUE.

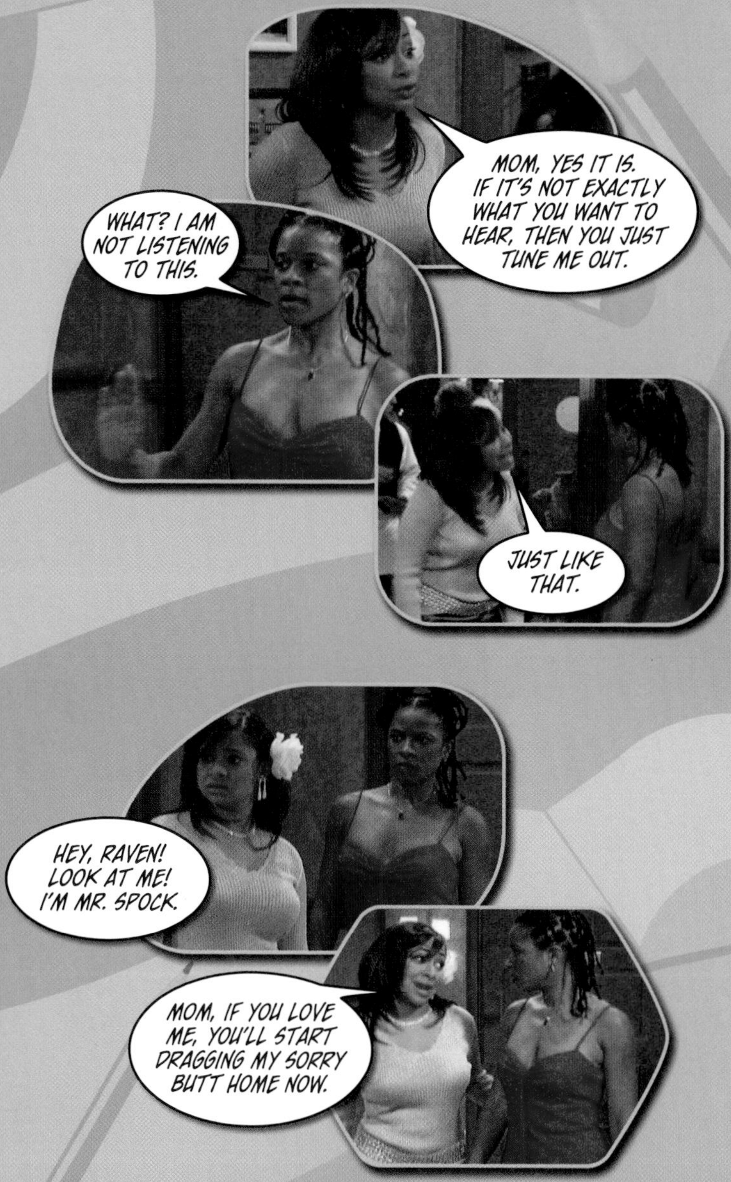
MOM, YES IT IS. IF IT'S NOT EXACTLY WHAT YOU WANT TO HEAR, THEN YOU JUST TUNE ME OUT.
WHAT? I AM NOT LISTENING TO THIS.
JUST LIKE THAT.
HEY, RAVEN! LOOK AT ME! I'M MR. SPOCK.
MOM, IF YOU LOVE ME, YOU'LL START DRAGGING MY SORRY BUTT HOME NOW.

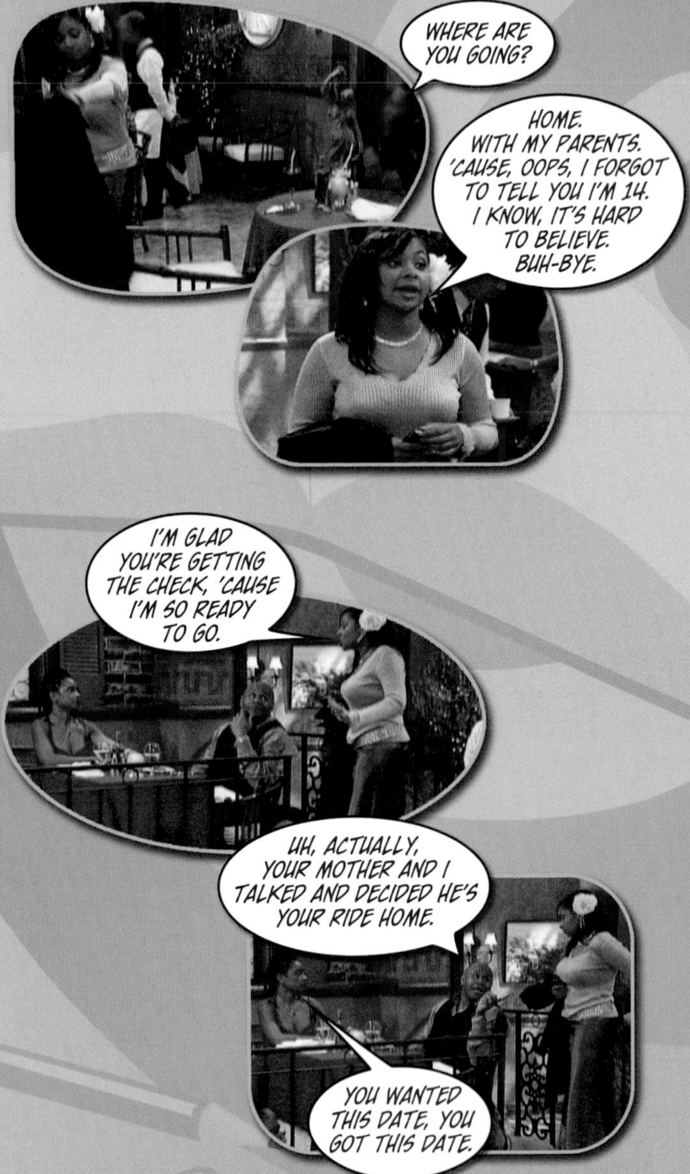
WHERE ARE YOU GOING?
HOME. WITH MY PARENTS. 'CAUSE, OOPS, I FORGOT TO TELL YOU I'M 14. I KNOW, IT'S HARD TO BELIEVE. BUH-BYE.
I'M GLAD YOU'RE GETTING THE CHECK, 'CAUSE I'M SO READY TO GO.
UH, ACTUALLY, YOUR MOTHER AND I TALKED AND DECIDED HE'S YOUR RIDE HOME.
YOU WANTED THIS DATE, YOU GOT THIS DATE.

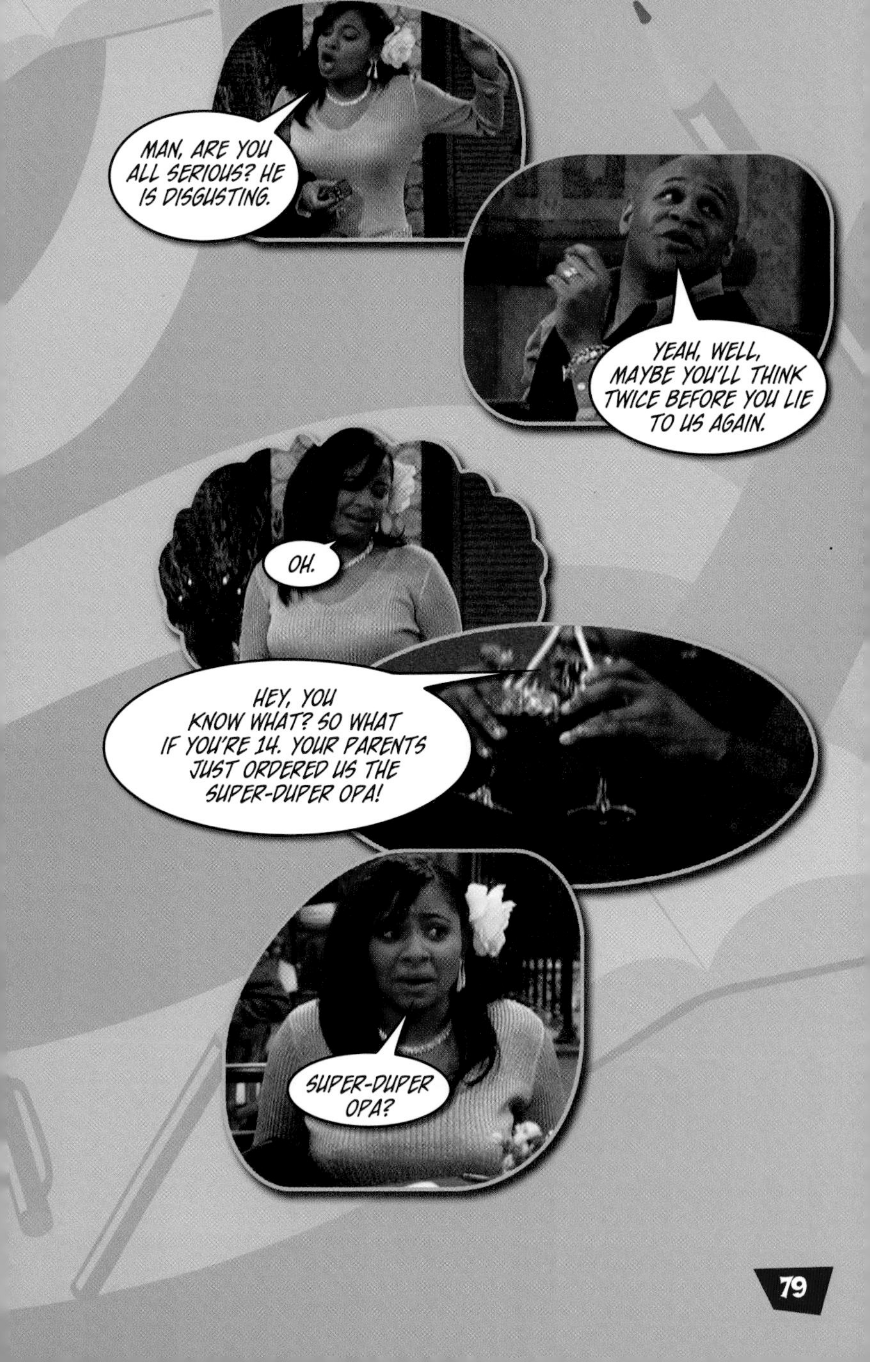
MAN, ARE YOU ALL SERIOUS? HE IS DISGUSTING.
YEAH, WELL, MAYBE YOU'LL THINK TWICE BEFORE YOU LIE TO US AGAIN.
OH.
HEY, YOU KNOW WHAT? SO WHAT IF YOU'RE 14. YOUR PARENTS JUST ORDERED US THE SUPER-DUPER OPA!
SUPER-DUPER OPA?

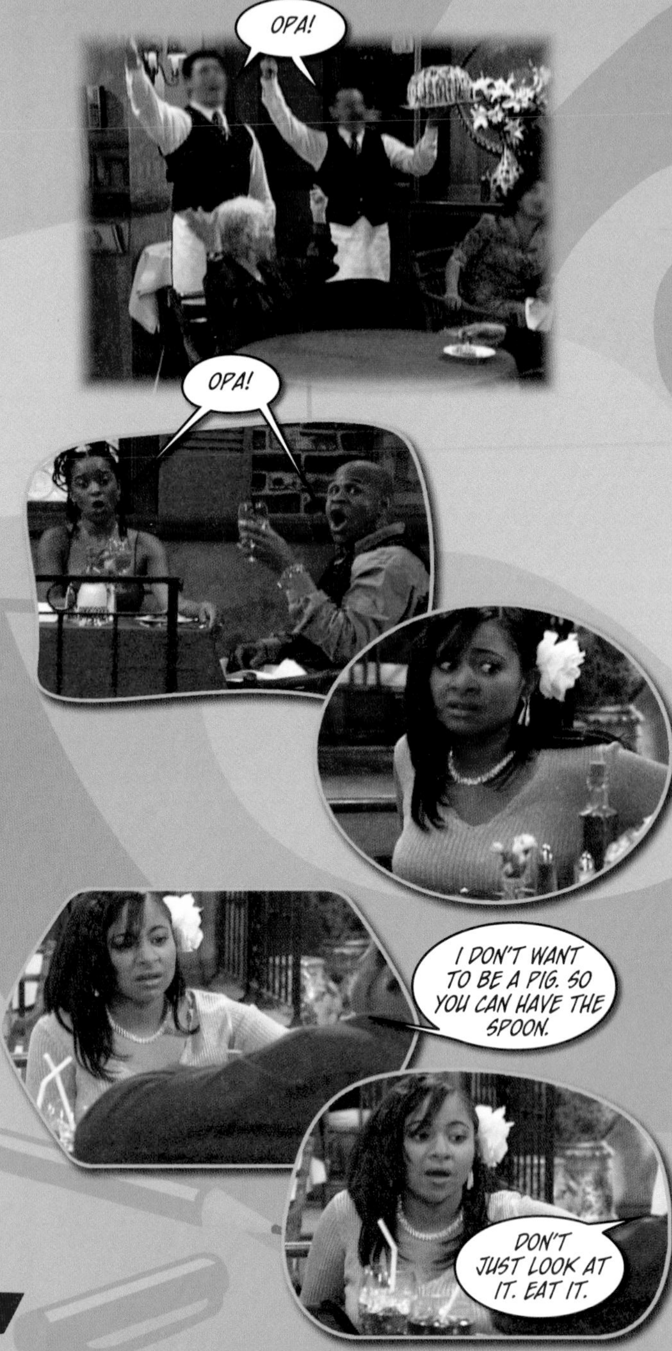
OPA!
OPA!
I DON'T WANT TO BE A PIG. SO YOU CAN HAVE THE SPOON.
DON'T JUST LOOK AT IT. EAT IT.

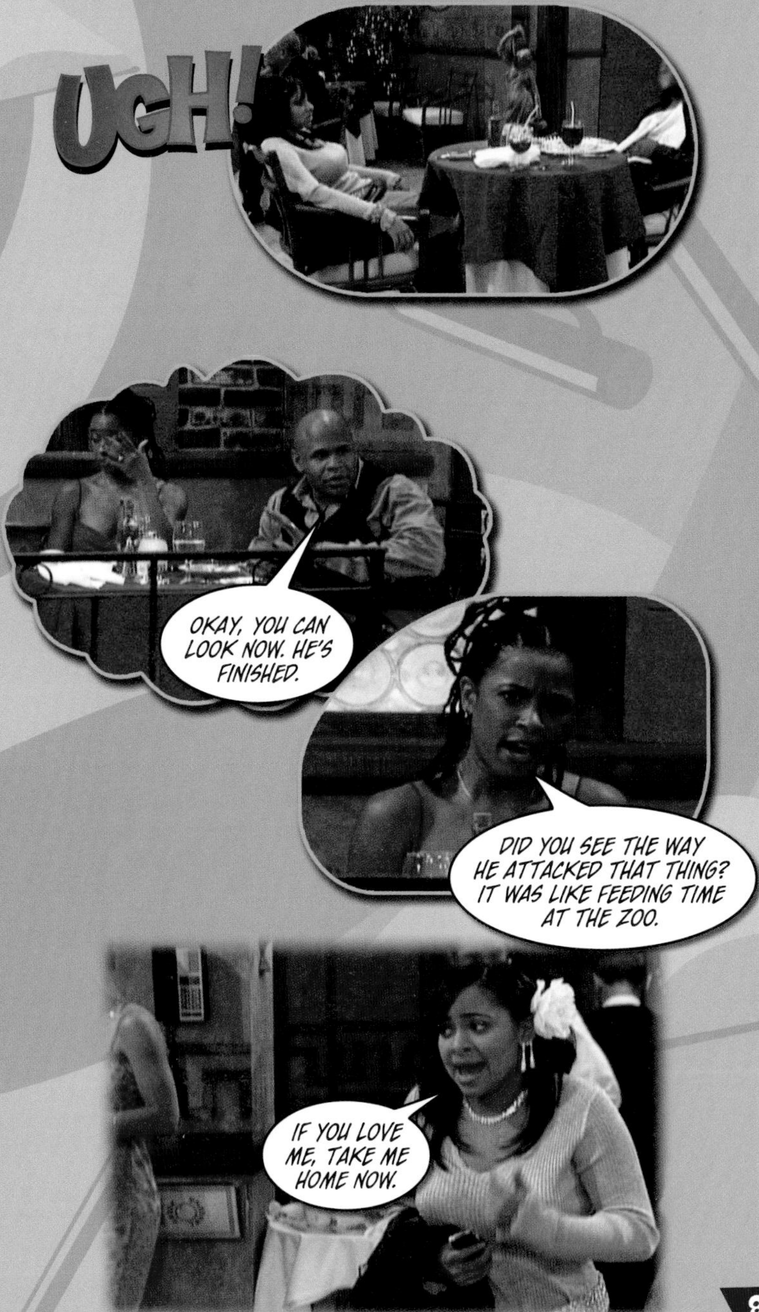
UGH!
OKAY, YOU CAN LOOK NOW. HE'S FINISHED.
DID YOU SEE THE WAY HE ATTACKED THAT THING? IT WAS LIKE FEEDING TIME AT THE ZOO.
IF YOU LOVE ME, TAKE ME HOME NOW.

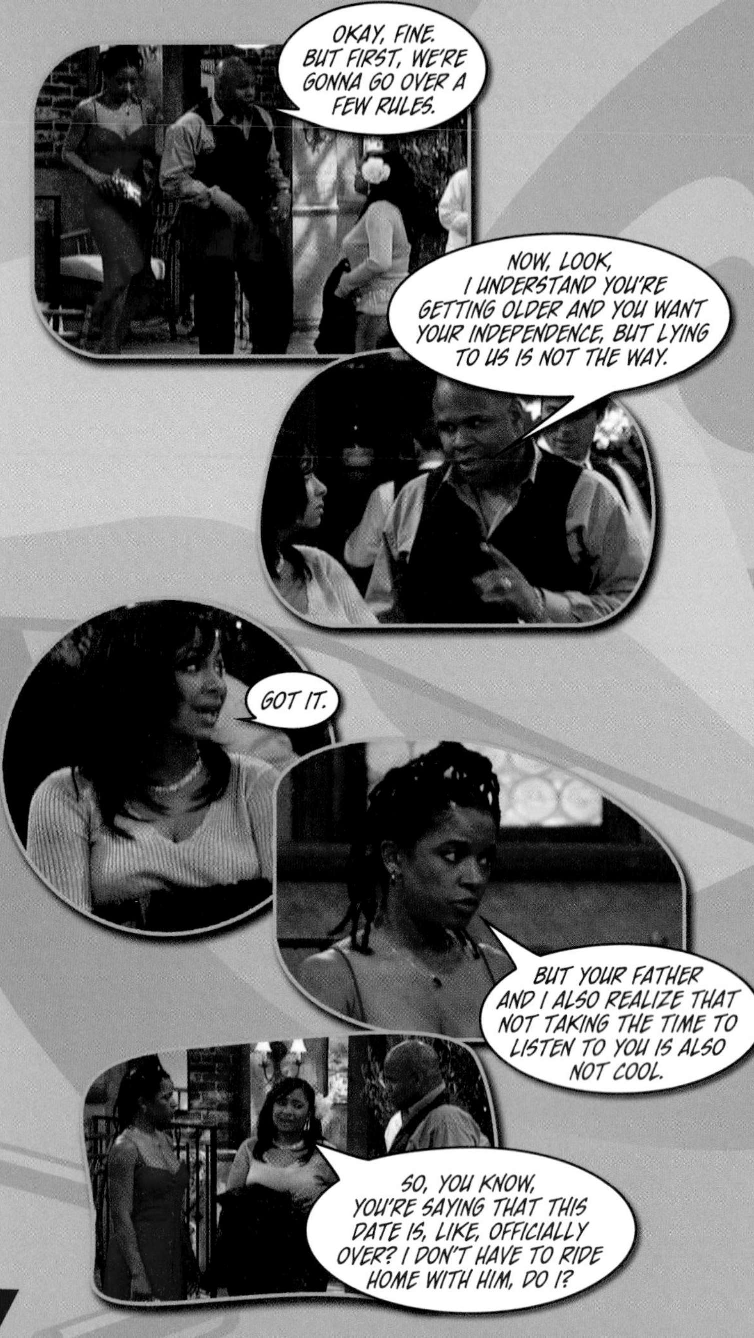
OKAY, FINE. BUT FIRST, WE'RE GONNA GO OVER A FEW RULES.
NOW, LOOK, I UNDERSTAND YOU'RE GETTING OLDER AND YOU WANT YOUR INDEPENDENCE, BUT LYING TO US IS NOT THE WAY.
GOT IT.
BUT YOUR FATHER AND I ALSO REALIZE THAT NOT TAKING THE TIME TO LISTEN TO YOU IS ALSO NOT COOL.
SO, YOU KNOW, YOU'RE SAYING THAT THIS DATE IS, LIKE, OFFICIALLY OVER? I DON'T HAVE TO RIDE HOME WITH HIM, DO I?

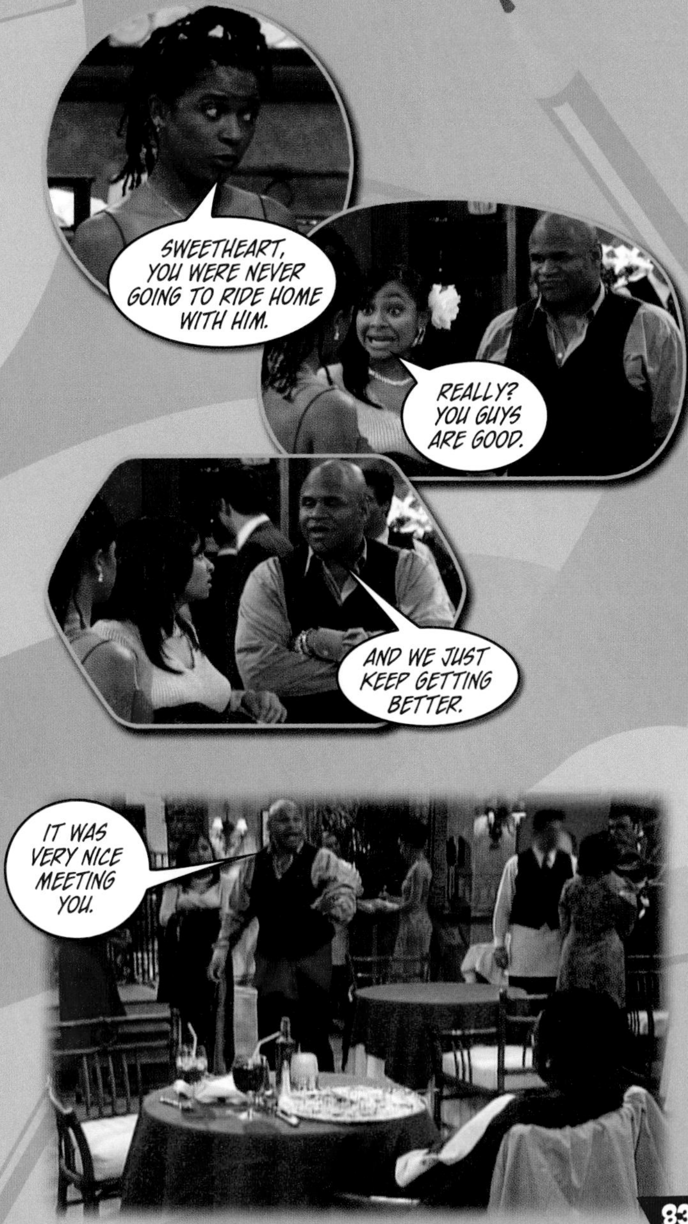
SWEETHEART, YOU WERE NEVER GOING TO RIDE HOME WITH HIM.
REALLY? YOU GUYS ARE GOOD.
AND WE JUST KEEP GETTING BETTER.
IT WAS VERY NICE MEETING YOU.

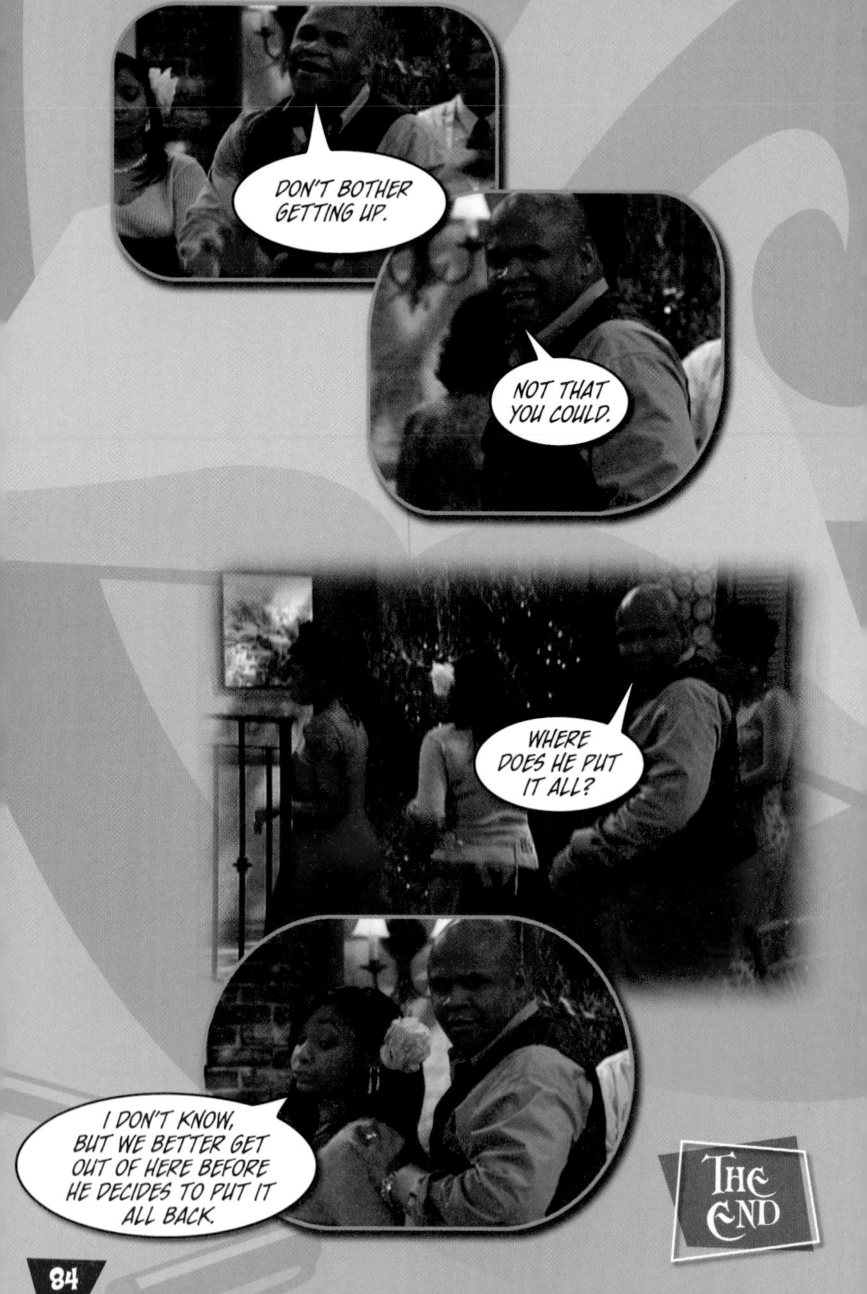
DON'T BOTHER GETTING UP.
NOT THAT YOU COULD.
WHERE DOES HE PUT IT ALL?
I DON'T KNOW, BUT WE BETTER GET OUT OF HERE BEFORE HE DECIDES TO PUT IT ALL BACK.
THE END

that's **SO** raven™

TOKYOPOP®

The future is now!

The hit show from Disney is
now a hot new Cine-Manga™!

A ALL AGES

www.**TOKYOPOP**.com

ALSO AVAILABLE FROM ☺ TOKYOPOP®

MANGA

.HACK//LEGEND OF THE TWILIGHT
ANGELIC LAYER
BABY BIRTH
BRAIN POWERED
BRIGADOON
B'TX
CANDIDATE FOR GODDESS, THE
CARDCAPTOR SAKURA
CARDCAPTOR SAKURA - MASTER OF THE CLOW
CHRONICLES OF THE CURSED SWORD
CLAMP SCHOOL DETECTIVES
CLOVER
COMIC PARTY
CORRECTOR YUI
COWBOY BEBOP
COWBOY BEBOP: SHOOTING STAR
CRAZY LOVE STORY
CRESCENT MOON
CROSS
CULDCEPT
CYBORG 009
D•N•ANGEL
DEMON DIARY
DEMON ORORON, THE
DIGIMON
DIGIMON TAMERS
DIGIMON ZERO TWO
DRAGON HUNTER
DRAGON KNIGHTS
DRAGON VOICE
DREAM SAGA
DUKLYON: CLAMP SCHOOL DEFENDERS
ET CETERA
ETERNITY
FAERIES' LANDING
FLCL
FLOWER OF THE DEEP SLEEP
FORBIDDEN DANCE
FRUITS BASKET
G GUNDAM
GATEKEEPERS
GIRL GOT GAME
GIRLS' EDUCATIONAL CHARTER
GUNDAM BLUE DESTINY
GUNDAM SEED ASTRAY
GUNDAM WING
GUNDAM WING: BATTLEFIELD OF PACIFISTS
GUNDAM WING: ENDLESS WALTZ

GUNDAM WING: THE LAST OUTPOST (G-UNIT)
HANDS OFF!
HARLEM BEAT
IMMORTAL RAIN
I.N.V.U.
INITIAL D
INSTANT TEEN: JUST ADD NUTS
JING: KING OF BANDITS
JING: KING OF BANDITS - TWILIGHT TALES
JULINE
KARE KANO
KILL ME, KISS ME
KINDAICHI CASE FILES, THE
KING OF HELL
KODOCHA: SANA'S STAGE
LEGEND OF CHUN HYANG, THE
MAGIC KNIGHT RAYEARTH I
MAGIC KNIGHT RAYEARTH II
MAN OF MANY FACES
MARMALADE BOY
MARS
MARS: HORSE WITH NO NAME
MINK
MIRACLE GIRLS
MODEL
MY LOVE
NECK AND NECK
ONE
ONE I LOVE, THE
PEACH GIRL
PEACH GIRL: CHANGE OF HEART
PITA-TEN
PLANET LADDER
PLANETES
PRINCESS AI
PSYCHIC ACADEMY
QUEEN'S KNIGHT, THE
RAGNAROK
RAVE MASTER
REALITY CHECK
REBIRTH
REBOUND
RISING STARS OF MANGA
SAILOR MOON
SAINT TAIL
SAMURAI GIRL REAL BOUT HIGH SCHOOL
SEIKAI TRILOGY, THE
SGT. FROG
SHAOLIN SISTERS

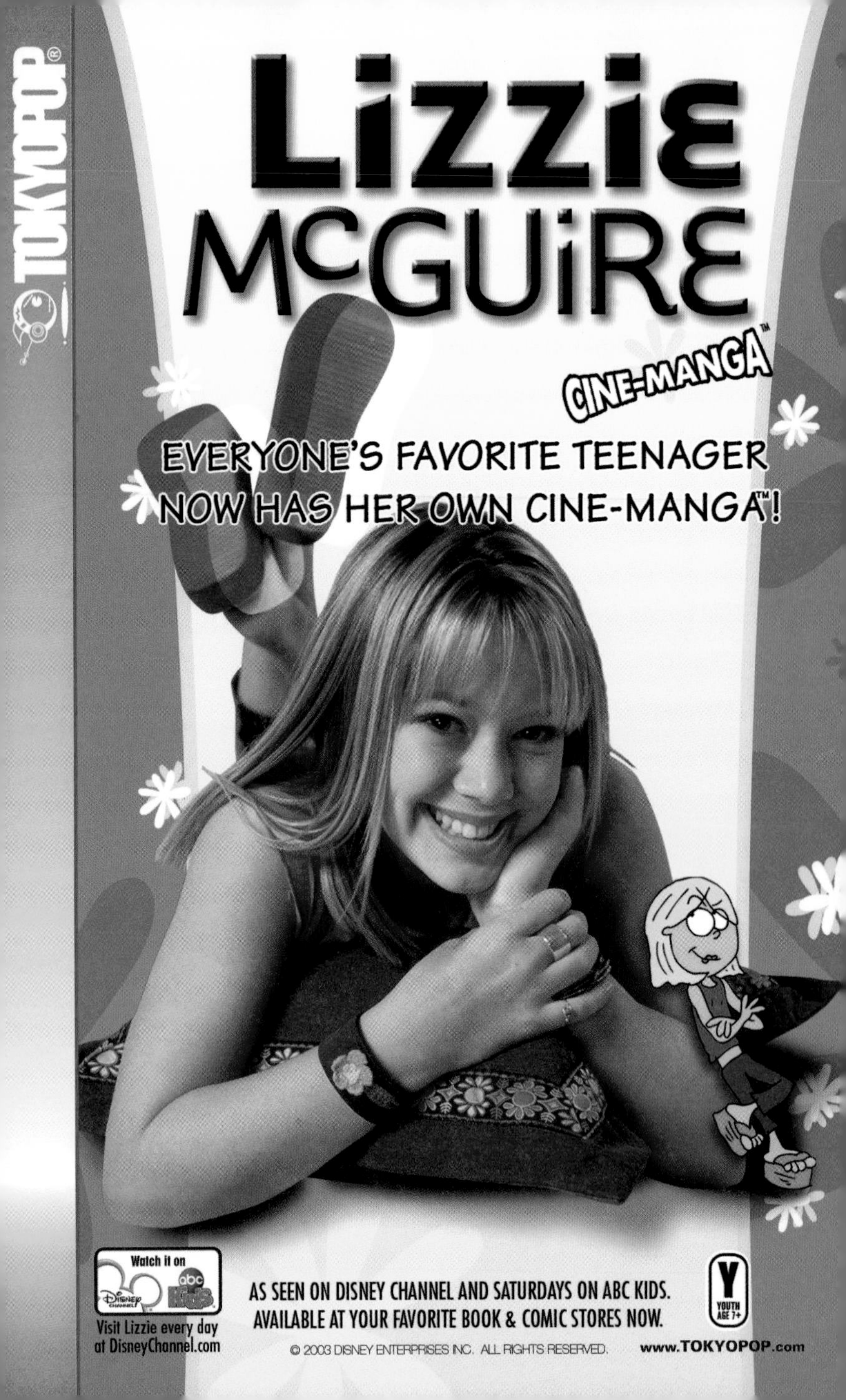
TOKYOPOP
Lizzie McGUIRE
CINE-MANGA™
EVERYONE'S FAVORITE TEENAGER NOW HAS HER OWN CINE-MANGA™!
Watch it on
Disney Channel
abc Kids
Visit Lizzie every day at DisneyChannel.com
AS SEEN ON DISNEY CHANNEL AND SATURDAYS ON ABC KIDS.
AVAILABLE AT YOUR FAVORITE BOOK & COMIC STORES NOW.
Y YOUTH AGE 7+
© 2003 DISNEY ENTERPRISES INC. ALL RIGHTS RESERVED.
www.TOKYOPOP.com

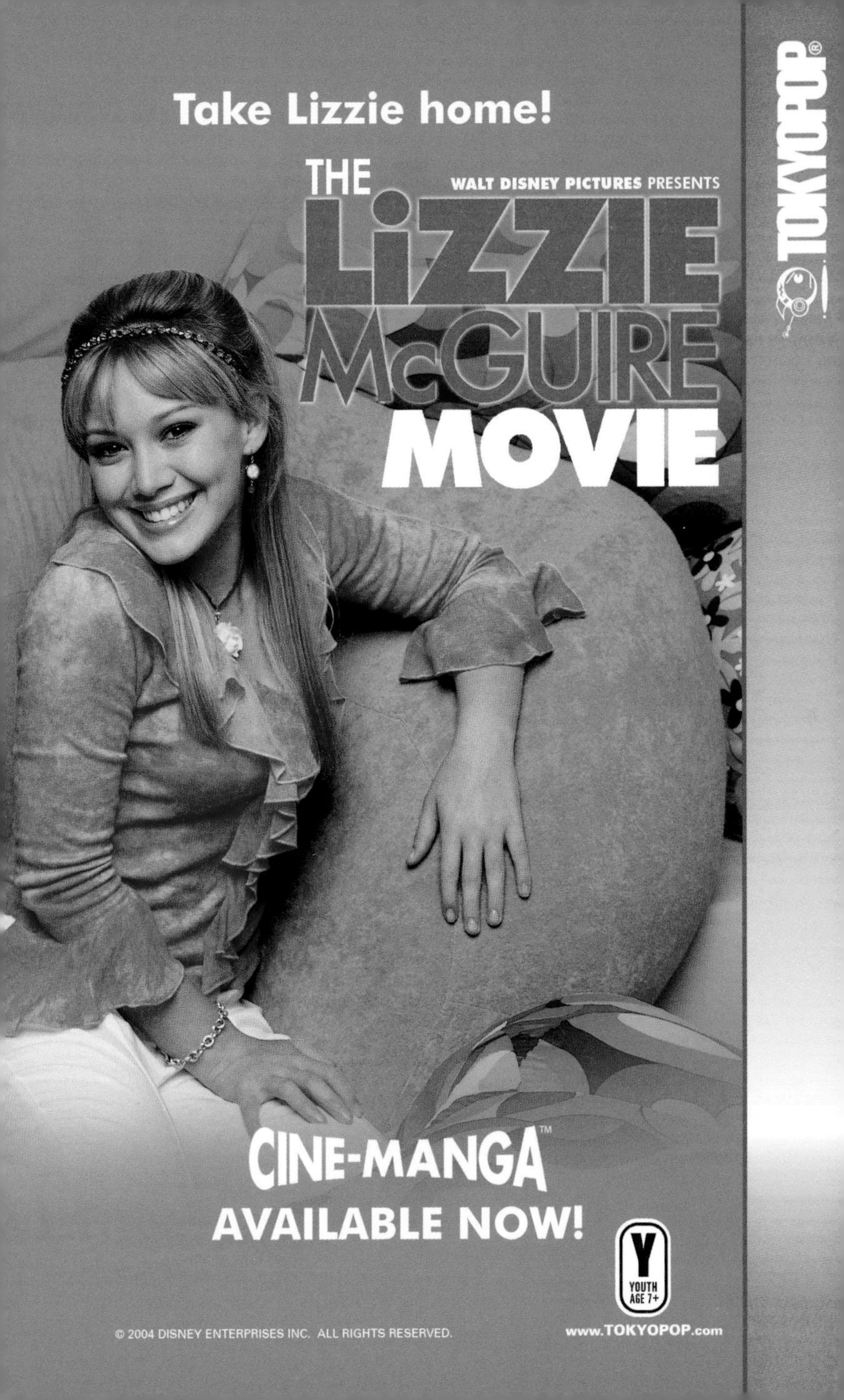
Take Lizzie home!
WALT DISNEY PICTURES PRESENTS
THE LIZZIE McGUIRE MOVIE
CINE-MANGA™
AVAILABLE NOW!
Y
YOUTH AGE 7+
© 2004 DISNEY ENTERPRISES INC. ALL RIGHTS RESERVED.
www.TOKYOPOP.com
TOKYOPOP®

GRAB YOUR FAVORITE SHOW AND GO!

DISNEY'S
KIM POSSIBLE

©Disney

Disney's hottest animated series just got a
Cine-Manga™ makeover...

Available at your favorite book & comic stores now!

Watch it on

Visit Kim every day at DisneyChannel.com

YOUTH
AGE 7+

www.TOKYOPOP.com

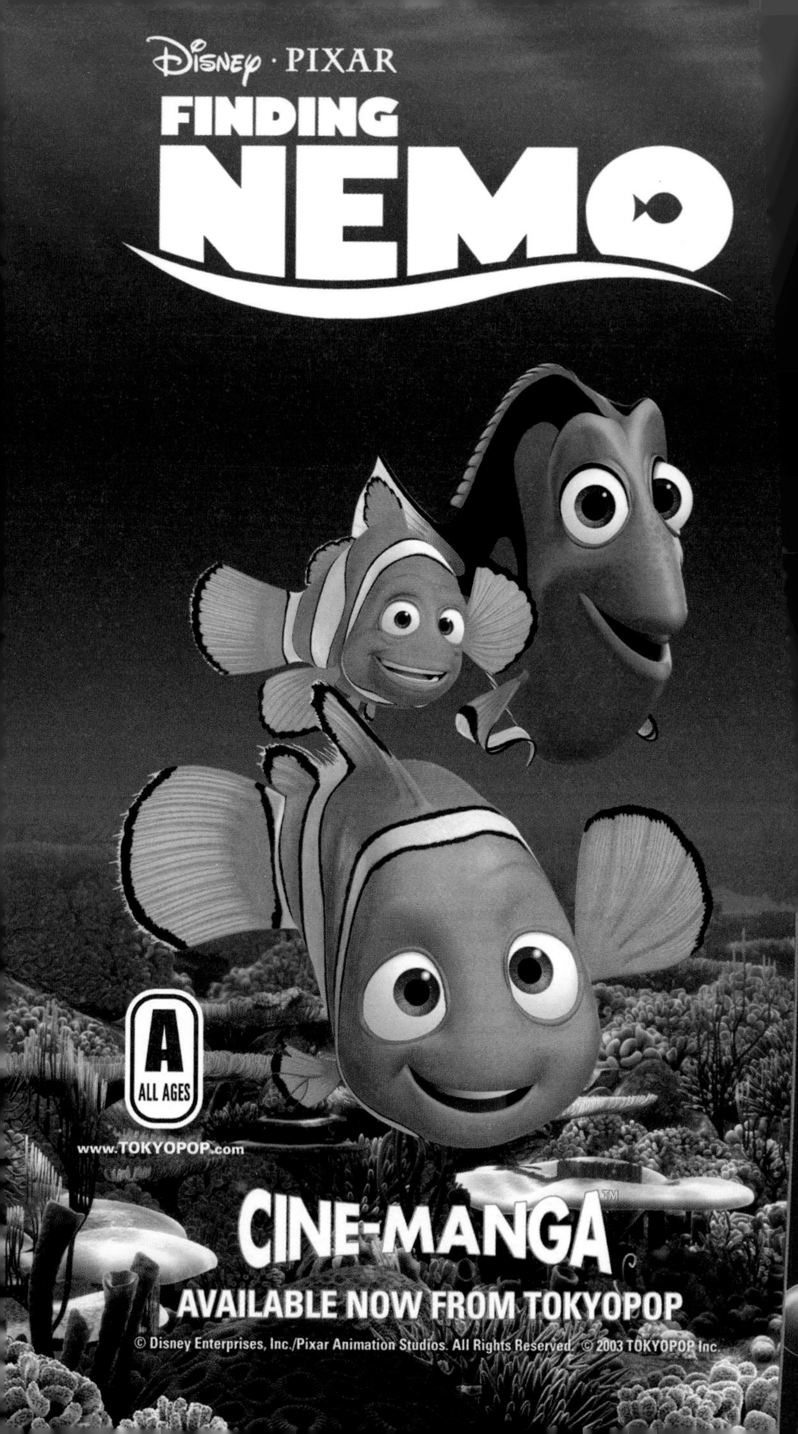
Disney · PIXAR
FINDING
NEMO
A
ALL AGES
www.TOKYOPOP.com
CINE-MANGA™
AVAILABLE NOW FROM TOKYOPOP
© Disney Enterprises, Inc./Pixar Animation Studios. All Rights Reserved. © 2003 TOKYOPOP Inc.

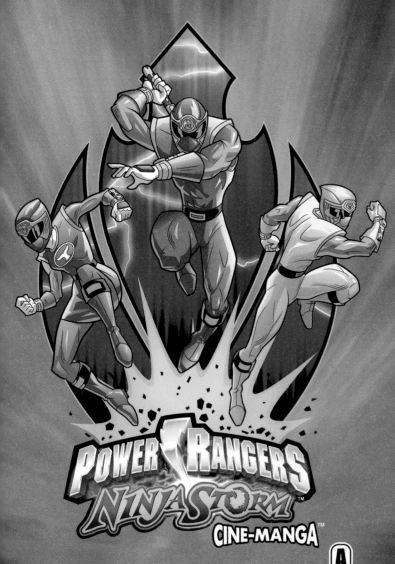

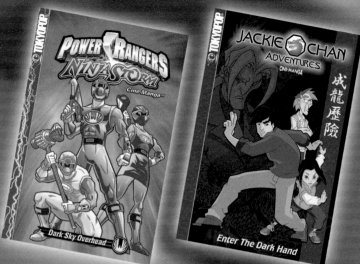

$7⁹⁹ SRP

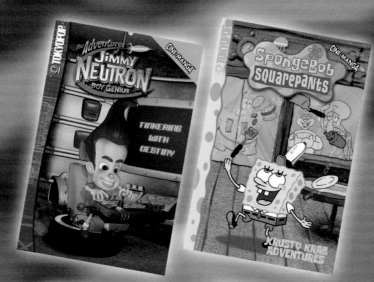

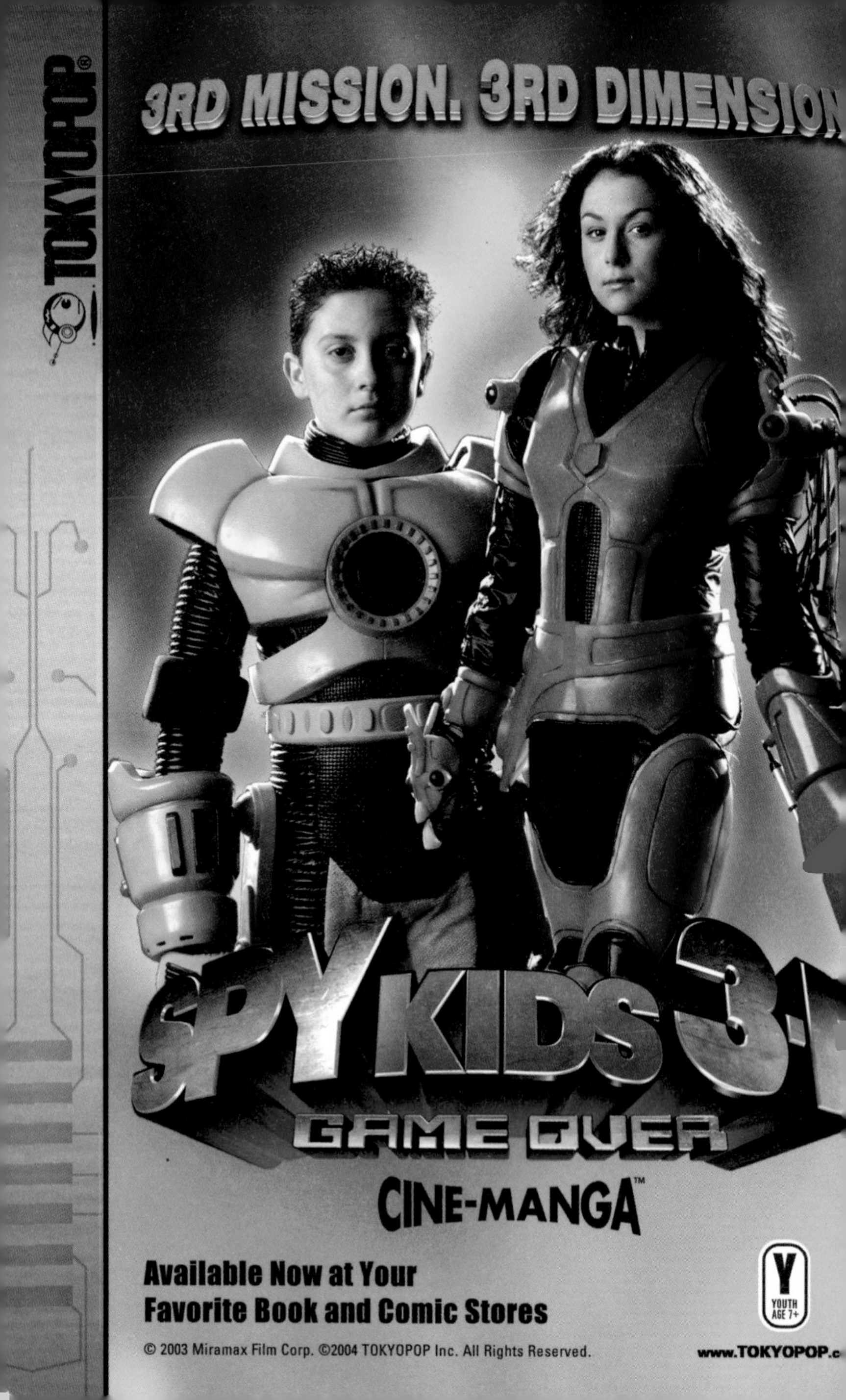
TOKYOPOP®
3RD MISSION. 3RD DIMENSION
SPY KIDS 3
GAME OVER
CINE-MANGA™
Available Now at Your
Favorite Book and Comic Stores
Y
YOUTH
AGE 7+
© 2003 Miramax Film Corp. ©2004 TOKYOPOP Inc. All Rights Reserved.
www.TOKYOPOP.c